GANGSTERS

&

WHORES

BY

G. S. WILLMOTT

CONTENTS

PINK FOR GIRLS

CHAPTER 1

SEPTEMBER 30, 1900
CAMBERWELL LONDON.

Ted Twiss was sitting at the kitchen table in his Hollington Street home, drinking his fourth glass of beer. He had been waiting for over two hours hoping to hear the sound of his son—or at least he hoped it would be his son—cry as newborn babies are meant to do.

Ted had just poured his fifth beer when he heard the sound he was yearning to hear, the cry of a baby. He left his glass and raced upstairs to the bedroom. He looked in, and there was his beloved wife cradling her newborn child.

'Congratulations Mr Twiss, you have a healthy baby girl,' said the midwife.

'A girl? What happened to the baby boy?'

He didn't approach his wife or look at his daughter. He went downstairs, grabbed his coat and headed for *The Ploughman's Arms* to brood over his misfortune.

That was how Matilda Twiss began her life; unwanted.

Matilda's suburb of Camberwell could be described as bipolar. At one end there were magnificent mansions and beautiful parks. Lawyers, doctors, bankers and businessmen lived in this section of Camberwell.

Matilda and her parents lived in the workingman's section where the housing was cramped, and the streets were dirty. It was known as one of London's notorious slums.

Hollington Street

Everybody, including her parents, called Matilda, Tilly. It was the name she would adopt for the remainder of her life.

Tilly had a reasonably normal life up until school age. Her father now accepted her and on occasion showed her some affection.

At age five Tilly attended the Lyndhurst Primary School. Although she was not the brightest child in the class she certainly wasn't the dumbest.

Tilly met a friend on the first day of school. Kate would remain Tilly's closest friend until they both left school at twelve. By the time the two girls had reached third grade they had established a reputation as bullies and standover merchants.

'Hey, Kate do you feel like a cream bun for lunch?'

'Too right Tilly I love cream buns. Where are we going to steal them?'

'I saw Sarah Jones with two of them in her lunch box. We'd better hurry before the fat little bitch shoves em down her cake hole.'

'Right let's go.'

The two girls headed for the school quadrangle in search of Sarah. They found her sitting on a bench talking to her friend Lucy. The lunch box was next to her with the contents waiting to be devoured.

'Sarah, hand over your lunch box. Kate and I fancy your cream buns.'

'I don't think so. I'm looking forward to eating them myself.'

Tilly approached the chubby girl, hitting her with a clenched fist in the face.

Lucy came to her friend's defence, but Kate kicked her in the stomach forcing Lucy to drop to her knees.

Tilly grabbed the lunch box and walked away with Kate. She turned back and yelled, 'The next time I ask politely for something from you, bitch, you better fucking give it me.'

Tilly and Kate laughed as they found a quiet spot to eat the buns. The lunch box with a sandwich and an apple still contained in it was thrown in a bin.

The two bullies ruled the schoolyard. Even some of the teachers were scared of them.

By the time they reached grade six, the final year of school, both Tilly and Kate had learned how to win favours from their male teachers. The most common practice was what they called "the gobble".

This practice would put them in good stead for their future occupations as prostitutes in The Strand.

LADIES OF THE NIGHT

DECEMBER 1914
THE STRAND LONDON

Tilly and Kate had decided long before they left school that working on their backs would be a hell of a lot better than working in an ammunition factory on their feet.

The First World War had begun in early August and despite the fact that many young men had enlisted and were now fighting overseas there were plenty of older men looking for the ultimate pleasure, particularly with young women.

Tilly and Kate were both still living at home when they began their new careers. Their parents approved on the basis that both girls contributed to the family budget.

The girls' regime encompassed eating dinner with the family then going to their bedrooms and applying makeup and dressing appropriately. Appropriately meant dressing like a tart. At ten pm the girls would make their way to The Strand where Tilly and Kate stood opposite *The Strand Hotel* hoping to attract a lonely guest. Both girls being fifteen certainly attracted their fair share of amorous old men.

Tilly watched the man approaching, dressed in a pinstripe suit and a bowler hat.

Here's a candidate if I ever saw one, she thought.

'Good evening young lady. May I inquire the amount you charge for your services?'

'Well, that, depends on how long you want with me and what you would like me to do.'

'What's the most common situation?'

'Most gentlemen prefer an hour and with that they get the full menu.'

'The full menu, pray tell; what is on the menu?'

'Darlin', you pay me £3, and you'll find out soon enough. What I will tell you is I've never had a complaint.'

'Jolly good. Why don't we go up to my room in The Strand?'

'If you like, but first things first— that'll be £3 thank you.'

Tilly looked over at Kate giving her a wink. Kate responded with thumbs up.

The gentleman paid Tilly the money and she accompanied him into the hotel, catching the lift to the third floor.

'So, what's your name darlin'?'

'Rupert.'

'My name is Tilly. I'm pleased to meet you. Now, Rupert, we need to get you undressed.'

'Yes, I might go to the bathroom.'

'Don't be shy, Rupert; after all we're going to get to know each other very well over the next little while. You just stand in front of me, and I'll take care of things.'

'If you say so, Tilly. As you can tell I'm a little nervous.'

Tilly took Rupert's coat and vest off and laid them on the chaise lounge. Next came his tie and shirt and finally his trousers, underwear and socks. Rupert stood in front of the young girl totally naked.

'Well, Rupert, I can see you're becoming a little excited sweetheart.'

Tilly took Rupert in her hands and began to stroke him gently, all the while looking in his eyes. Rupert's legs began to quiver.

'Rupert, would you like me to suck you darlin'? I have a reputation for being the best gobbler on The Strand.'

All Rupert could manage was, 'Yes thank you.'

Tilly took him into her warm wet mouth, sucking him until he couldn't hold on any more.

'Well, Rupe, that didn't take very long. Let me clean up and then we can move onto the second course.'

Tilly led her client by the hand to the bed, instructing him to lie on his back. She straddled the bewildered banker and rode him for what seemed an eternity. Just when he thought he would ejaculate again Tilly stopped and dismounted; she knelt on the bed and instructed Rupert to enter her from behind. This is how the lovemaking concluded with Rupert coming for the second time.

Tilly went to the bathroom and then dressed. She entered the hotel room only to find Rupert snoring.

She reached over the bed and kissed her client on the forehead and departed.

As she headed back to the street she smiled to herself. *I really have a great job. I do love fucking.*

Tilly's aim was to have up to ten customers a night and being young and attractive made this number more than achievable.

Tilly returned to the corner of The Strand and Exeter Street to wait for her next client. It was 11 pm, with plenty of time left.

Kate wasn't on the corner she must have been with a client Tilly thought. She didn't have to wait long when a very large gentleman approached her.

'Good evening young lady would you care to make an old man very happy?'

'Hello darling, yes, I can make you happy if you pay me the right money.'

'How much am I required to pay you?'

'I think £5 for an hour would be about right.'

'My goodness, you don't come cheaply, do you?'

'That's right, sweetheart, I don't come cheaply.'

'Fair enough. Would you care to accompany me to my hotel room?'

'Yes darling, of course— just hand over the fiver and we can be on our way.'

The fat man reached into his coat and extracted a large leather wallet. He pulled out a £5 note and passed it to the young woman.

'Right, let's go and have some fun,' said Tilly.

They entered The Strand and rode the lift to the fourth floor. Once inside his room Tilly undressed the obese man and instructed him to lie on his back on the bed. This was how Tilly earned her fee for there was no way he was going to get on top of her.

Despite the client paying for an hour the lovemaking lasted only thirty minutes before he was snoring so loudly Tilly thought he'd crack the ceiling plaster. She cleaned herself and left quietly, but not before she stole another £5 from his wallet. This wasn't the first time she had stolen money from a sleeping client's wallet, and it wouldn't be the last.

Tilly's life of crime was about to be taken to a new level.

When she returned to her corner she found Kate. Both had enjoyed a profitable night. The two ladies of the night decided to call it quits after all they had serviced ten clients each they went home and got some much-needed sleep.

They walked along Walworth Road heading for Camberwell.

After ten minutes of walking, Tilly noticed a drunk staggering along in the opposite direction. Tilly hit him as hard as she could in the stomach, and he moaned and slumped to the footpath. Both girls kicked him several times. Tilly leaned over the poor wretch and took his wallet. Tilly then kicked him hard in the groin and both girls left him writhing on the footpath. Tilly and Kate began to laugh.

'Well, that was better than servicing a client. Look Kate, we scored £30.'

'Nice easy money,' replied Kate.

Tilly took every opportunity to steal money, whether it was from clients or drunks in the street. This behaviour became the norm for the remainder of her life, stealing, violence and intimidation.

THE AUSSIE DIGGER

CHAPTER 3

DECEMBER 1916

Tilly was standing at her usual corner down the road from the Strand Hotel when she noticed a soldier swaggering towards her. His hat gave away his nationality. It was a slouch hat, so he was an Australian.

'G'day love, fancy a little slap and tickle with a true-blue Aussie soldier?'

'I've had plenty of Australians. What makes you so special?'

'I'll show you if you like.'

'You show me your three quid first, sweetheart.'

'Blimey, that's a bit rich. How about £2?'

'I don't negotiate. If you want me, you pay me.'

'All right here's your money; you better be good.'

'Oh, I'm good, very good. Where are you staying?'

'At the Strand.'

'Right, nice and handy; let's go.'

Tilly took the soldier's arm and they headed for the hotel.

'So what's your name, darling?'

'Jim, Jim Devine.'

'Devine by name Devine by nature, hey?'

'You got it, love.'

They reached Jim's room on the second floor. Tilly had seen more salubrious rooms in the Strand, but it had all the essentials.

'So, Jim Devine, what do you fancy, love?'

'Why don't you surprise me, Tilly? I like surprises.'

The young woman used all her skills and experience to make Big Jim a very happy digger.

After the session they both lay on the bed. This was something Tilly rarely did as the norm was to finish, wash up and get down to her corner to grab the next client.

But she found Jim different. He was interesting; maybe it was the fact he was Australian.

'Jim, what's Australia like?'

'It's God's own earth Tilly, always warm with beautiful beaches. Wide open pastures where wheat and sheep are grown. I own the largest kangaroo farm in the country.'

'Kangaroos, I didn't know you could farm bloody kangaroos.'

'Yep, I provide meat for pet food and the skins for leather.'

'That sounds wonderful, Jim. I wish I could visit your farm one day.'

'You never know, Tilly, you never know.'

Finally, Tilly got dressed and bade her Aussie client farewell.

She saw Kate standing on the corner and approached her with enthusiasm.

'Hello, Kate I just fucked an Australian digger. Geez he was nice. He knew how to do it as well. What do you know about Australia?'

'I have an aunt and uncle who immigrated there a few years ago and apparently they love it.'

'Where in Australia do they live?'

'Sydney.'

'This bloke, Jim, lives out in the bush on his kangaroo farm part of the time and in Sydney for the rest of his time.'

'Tilly you sound like you've fallen for this bloke.'

'I'm not sure about fallen but I like him.'

The two young ladies decided it was time to retire for the night and made their way home.

The Twiss family were gathered around the breakfast table the following morning. Ted, Tilly's father, inquired how much money his daughter had made in the past week.

Tilly knew she needed to contribute to the family's finances, but she also knew there was no way she would divulge her true earnings.

'I made £10 Dad. It was a slow week— not many soldiers in town.'

'Fair enough, girl. Well you keep £2, and the rest can keep the family fed and housed.'

Ted worked as a bricklayer for £2 a week so an additional £8 was most welcome. A reasonable amount of Tilly's earnings would be spent down the pub.

Tilly's actual earnings were £20 so she was doing pretty well.

The next night was Saturday which was usually a girl's busiest night. Tilly had already entertained five clients despite it being only 11 pm.

Standing on her corner she saw a tall gentleman dressed in a dark suit walking towards her. She was hoping it would be her next and final client.

'Hello darling, what do you fancy?'

'Hello, Tilly don't you remember me?'

'Jim, of course I remember you; it's not every day a girl gets fucked by a kangaroo farmer. Have you come back for some more?'

'Well, as a matter of fact I was hoping you might like to join me for a drink down at Soho once you've finished for the night.'

'I'd love to, Jim. I can finish up now if you like.'

'Beauty! Let's go.'

Tilly put her arm through her escort's as they walked to a taxi rank. The trip took only a few minutes. Jim chose his favourite drinking spot; *The Bohemian.*

'What would care to drink, Tilly?'

'I'll have a whisky, thank you.'

'You have expensive tastes for a young girl don't you?'

'You should know I'm an expensive girl.'

'I suppose I should. One whisky coming up.'

Tilly and Jim sat in a booth at the back of the pub

The first question Tilly asked Jim was about Australia; she was fascinated with the southern continent.

'Tilly, I honestly believe it's God's own country. It has everything, including gold, wheat, sheep and kangaroos.'

'It sounds wonderful,' Tilly said wistfully. 'I wish I could go there.'

'As I said when I first met you, you never know—you might just get there.'

'What did you do in the Great War?'

'The fucking war is what I prefer to call it. I was what they call a sapper. That means I dug trenches and tunnels all bloody day. Mind you, I'd prefer that to being in the infantry. Those poor bastards were in the firing line.'

'Well at least we won the bloody war thank God. I didn't fancy being under the heel of the Kaiser and his cronies.'

'No, that wouldn't have been too good.'

For the next three months Tilly and Jim were an item, drinking and sometimes fighting in the Soho bars until all hours.

On one particular night Jim proposed to the sixteen-year-old and she accepted at once. Jim arranged to meet with Tilly's father Ted to ask for her hand in marriage.

Ted agreed, although he was concerned with the proposed reduction in income coming into the household.

Tilly would soon be moving to the land of milk and honey.

DEVINE SAPPER

CHAPTER 4

JANUARY 1915

Jim Devine had just returned from Bathurst where he had been stationed for the past three months shearing sheep for various sheep stations in and around the area. He was feeling happy with himself. He had a wallet full of cash and was looking forward to spending it on beer and women.

He was sitting at the bar at *The Tradesman's Arms* consuming his sixth schooner when an old mate entered the bar.

'G'day Big Jim. I'm surprised to find you in here, you scoundrel.'

'Why would you say that Bob? You know it's me pub.'

'I heard the cops are looking for you. The word is you were behind the robbery at the Drummond Jewellery store.'

'That's bullshit and they fucking know it. They're always trying to nab me for stuff I never done.'

'Well, either way, mate, I'd keep me head down for a while.'

'Yeah, I suppose you're right Bob, although there's not that many places to hide out.'

Mate, I've just enlisted in the army. They're desperate for new recruits and they pay you six bob a day. Not only that I get to see a bit of the world—you know, England, France and so on. Why don't you join me?'

'Geez, that doesn't sound half bad. The only thing is I might get shot by a fucking German.'

'Mate, I reckon it's just as dangerous hanging around Darlinghurst what with all the gangs and such. It also gets you away from the fucking cops for a while.'

'You know what Bob; I think you're right. I'll think about it. Where in the hell do I sign up if I decide to join?

'At the Paddington Barracks just down the road.'

Jim finished his beer and returned to his room over number 56 Palmer Street. He sorted out a few private matters, burned some toast, drank a lukewarm cup of tea and went to bed.

By the next morning, he had made his decision. He headed to the Paddington Barracks to join up to fight for King and country.

The line seemed to go on forever. Obviously enlisting was a popular thing to do. Finally, Jim was next in line, and he approached the officer at the desk.

'Right, what's your name?'

'James Devine.'

'You may not be in the army yet, but you address me as sir. Is that clear?'

'Yes, sir.'

'Good. Occupation?'

'Shearer, sir.'

The officer wrote down all of Jim's details on a standard army form.

'I'll get you to join that line over there for a medical check-up. If you pass that you are in the army. Good luck.'

Jim joined the line and an hour later he stepped up to a doctor dressed in a white coat. Jim passed the medical without a hitch and was directed to the third and final desk. He signed the necessary forms and was directed into another large room where he was fitted out for his uniform.

He had been assigned to the 1st Tunnelling Company as a sapper.

Jim departed from the barracks unsure if he was happy, as he had never responded well to authority even in primary school, the highest level of his education.

He arrived back at his room to find his mate Bob waiting for him outside his door.

'Well, Jim how'd you go, cobber?'

'I'm in, mate. They put me in a tunnelling company as a sapper. Sounds as if I'll be using a shovel rather than a Lee Enfield rifle.'

'Mate, that's not such a bad thing— at least you'll be out of the firing line. As for me, I'm in the fucking infantry.'

FEBRUARY 15, 1915

Jim was instructed to report to the Holsworthy Army Camp near Liverpool for six weeks basic training.

Holsworthy Army Camp

It was here he learned to march, polish his boots and dig holes. In the last week the sappers were given weapons training in case they may need to fire a rifle in anger.

Jim did manage to stay out of trouble during his training… not something he was known for while serving on the Western Front.

APRIL 15, 1915

Jim and the 1st Tunnelling Company embarked on to the *S.S Ceramic* bound for Egypt where they would initially be stationed. The voyage would take six weeks, most of which would be taken up by boredom and two-up, a gambling game played with two pennies.

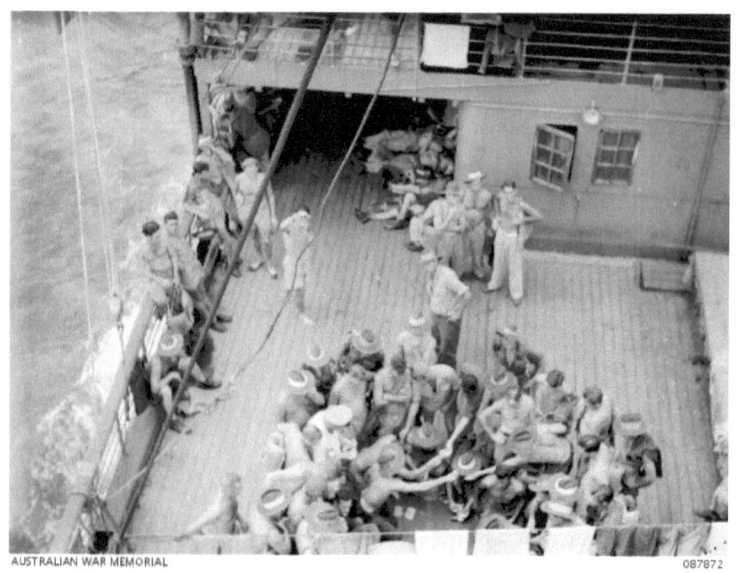

AUSTRALIAN WAR MEMORIAL   087872

A Game of Two-Up on the Ceramic

It didn't take Jim long to find trouble when he accused another soldier of cheating and beat him to an inch of his life. The MPs dragged Jim away locking him up in the brig. The unfortunate soldier spent two weeks in the ship's hospital. Jim was sentenced to four weeks in the brig. This was Jim's first taste of military discipline and was not to be his last.

JUNE 2, 1915

The *SS Ceramic* docked at the port of Alexandria in the morning but by the time the diggers disembarked it was 2 pm and a stifling 100 degrees.

'Fucking hell! How hot can it get in this stinking place?' asked Jim.

'I hope not much hotter,' said Dave, Jim's new mate he had shared his time with in the brig.

The Australian troops were ordered to march to the railway station where they were crammed into hot and smelly carriages for the journey to Cairo.

Three hours later the train and its passengers pulled into the main station in Cairo. The diggers were hoping they could now rest but after an hour's break, and a snack of cheese and bread they were ordered to march to Mena Camp three hours away.

Mena Camp

Jim and his mates had only seen pictures of the pyramids before, and now they were camping in their shadow.

Jim and his company had hardly settled into Mena Camp when they received orders to march to the Cairo Railway Station where they would retrace the route back to Alexandria, where their favourite troop ship the *SS Ceramic* was waiting to take them to Marseilles in France.

Once they arrived in Marseilles they boarded a train, which would take them up to the Western Front. The real work was about to begin for Jim and his comrades.

JUNE 10, 1916
FROMELLES

The 1ˢᵗ Australian Tunnelling Company were assigned the task to dig adequate trenches along the Allied line facing the German defences in preparation for an attack.

'This is fucking hopeless, Bob, every time we dig down the fucking trench gets filled with water. How in the fuck are we going to be able to get down far enough?'

'Yeah, I know what you mean. Let's hope the brass will have enough sense to abandon their plan.'

One officer, Brigadier General Pompey Elliot, observed the difficulty the sappers were having, and he ordered sandbags to be placed on top of the parapet to give the diggers cover. The digging ceased.

Fromelles was the first major battle fought by Australian troops on the Western Front. Directed against a strong German position known as the Sugar Loaf salient, the attack was intended primarily as a feint to draw German troops away from the Somme offensive then being pursued further to the south. A seven-hour preparatory bombardment deprived the attack of any hope of surprise and ultimately proved ineffective in subduing the well-entrenched defenders. When the troops of the 5th Australian and 61st British Divisions attacked at 6 pm on 19 July 1916, they suffered heavily at the hands of German machine-gunners. Small parts of the German trenches were captured by the 8th and 14th Australian Brigades, but, devoid of flanking support and subjected to fierce counter-attacks, they were forced to withdraw. By 8 am on 20 July 1916, the battle was over. The 5th Australian Division suffered 5,533 casualties, rendering it incapable of offensive action for many months; the 61st British Division suffered 1,547. The German casualties were little more than 1,000. The attack was a complete failure as the Germans realised within a few hours it was merely a feint. It, therefore, had no impact whatsoever on the progress of the Somme offensive.

Australian War Memorial

Jim and Bob survived the carnage of Fromelles, and the company was assigned a new task, which would take a year to complete.

FLANDERS, BELGIUM 1916

General Haig was studying a report written by Major Norton-Griffiths, an engineer of high renown. Prior to the war, Norton-Griffiths had owned an engineering company that had built tunnels in Britain and also in South Africa and Australia. His company was given the task of blowing up oil wells in Romania to stop the Germans getting their hands on the precious commodity.

Major Norton-Griffiths

Major Norton-Griffiths had written a report to General Plumer recommending he and a team of engineers together with hand-picked sappers tunnel under the German lines and fill them with explosives with the objective of blowing the Germans to kingdom come. This, he ascertained, would allow the Allied forces to attack and take the high ridge of Messines thus securing the Ypres salient.

General Plumer requested a meeting with General Haig to discuss the plan, while Norton-Griffiths accompanied him.

'So you think this plan will work, do you, General Plumer?'

'Yes, sir, I have gone over it thoroughly with Major Norton-Griffiths and I am sure it will work. The Major has extensive tunnelling experience and the methods devised by his company will mean the noise levels will be kept to a minimum, so the Germans won't hear a damn thing, not until the explosions go off anyway. They call it "clay-kicking".'

'Major Norton-Griffiths, I take it that you will be the officer in charge of the digging operation?' asked General Haig.

'Yes, sir, I believe I will report directly to General Plumer.'

'How are you going to recruit experienced diggers from the ranks, Major?'

'Sir, I have hired many men in my engineering company before the war. I know what to look for.'

'General Plumer, I will approve this plan. Make sure it works.'

'It will, sir, I assure you.'

General Plumer and Norton-Griffiths left General Haig's office, taking a seat in the Major's black Rolls Royce. The car was pristine when Major Norton-Griffiths arrived in France, but it was looking a little worse for wear now.

They were pleased that General Haig had approved their plan but were very conscious of the long hard road in front of them.

'So, Norton-Griffiths, how are you going to convince the various commanders to release their men to go and dig clay?'

'I think I know how to do it, sir.'

They arrived back at General Plumer's Headquarters and agreed to meet the next day to finalise the location and size of the mines they were going to lay.

Once they agreed on the plan, it was up to Major Norton-Griffiths to recruit the men needed.

Norton-Griffiths (on the right) with his Rolls Royce

He loaded up the Rolls with several cases of Château Lafitte Rothschild wine, which he had collected since landing in France.

He then drove around to various units hoping to convince the commanders to release their men with engineering experience.

He pulled up at the command post of Major John Davies.

'Hello, Major, I was wondering if we could have a chat?'

'Why not, come on in to my luxurious dugout,' he said in jest.

'I have a proposition for you.'

'Yes, and what would that be, Major?'

'I need men with good engineering experience for a very important mission. I believe you have two such men in your company.'

'Do I? And who would they be?'

'Corporals Smyth and Pittard.'

'I don't think so, Major. They are two of my best men. Out of the question.'

'Well, may I suggest six bottles of Château Lafitte may encourage you to release them into my care?'

'You're joking. Where did you find those?'

'Well, you can find them in the boot of my car. Never mind where I found them.'

'All right, Major, you have yourself a deal.'

'Excellent.'

Major Norton-Griffiths used this tactic to ensure he had all the experienced men he needed for the project.

At the completion of his recruitment drive, he had recruited many miners from Britain, Australia, Canada and New Zealand.

General Plumer kept a very close watch on the tunnelling and after eighteen months of digging, the twenty-two mines were ready to explode.

The objective of the attack was Messines Ridge, southeast of Ypres, a town the Germans had tried to occupy since 1914. The British knew they had to capture the Ridge before they could mount a much larger attack on Passchendaele, in the Third Battle of Ypres.

General Plumer and his officers had been planning this attack for over eighteen months, reflecting Plumer's nature as a meticulous planner, who left nothing to chance.

He commissioned the laying of twenty-two mineshafts underneath the German lines running along the ridge. The plan was to detonate all twenty-two at the same time, at 3.10am on the 7th of June 1917. Prior to the bombs going off, they would hit the Germans with artillery. They would then attack the Germans with infantry attacks. Tanks and gas would support the infantry.

The 1st Australian Tunnelling Company was given the task of tunnelling under what was known as Hill 60. Jim and his company worked tirelessly to complete the task.

One of the mines was discovered by the Germans and destroyed, while two others were detonated by the British as they were outside the field of the attack.

The Germans were also tunnelling frantically and on more than one occasion each side would encounter the other deep below and deadly hand-to-hand fighting would take place.

The British started shelling the Germans on the 21st of May, using two thousand, three hundred heavy guns and three hundred heavy mortars. The bombardment ceased at 2.50am on the 7th of June. The Germans knew the British modus operandi and, sensing an imminent attack, rushed to their defensive positions, with machine guns manned and flares launched to see if there was any British movement.

There was complete silence for twenty minutes. The Germans were increasingly nervous, then at 3.10 am the order was given to detonate the mines, which totalled six hundred tons of explosive. Nineteen mines exploded.

The mines blew the crest off Messines Ridge. People reported hearing the explosions in Dublin, and the Prime Minister of the day, Lloyd George, heard it at number 10 Downing Street. No greater explosion created by mankind had ever happened and didn't happen again until the atomic bomb was dropped on Hiroshima.

Mine Crater at Hill 60

The effect on the German defenders was devastating. It was estimated that the explosion alone killed 10,000 men. The objective was taken in three hours.

There were two unexploded mines on the day, and they were due to be dismantled, but they were left behind as the British went on to Passchendaele without really worrying about them. The documents describing where they were laid got destroyed in later battles, so they were never dismantled. Nobody knew exactly where they were, and it wasn't until 1955 that one exploded during a thunderstorm. There were no real casualties apart from a cow. The remaining mine still lies dormant and everybody in the general area hopes it stays that way.

The Battle of Messines was a great morale booster for the Allies and for the first time, the defensive German casualties of 25,000 exceeded the 17,000 Allied troops.

Messines was the highlight of Private James Devine's military career—several detentions for Absence Without Leave were not.

MISS YOU BABE

CHAPTER 5

APRIL 12, 1917

At the Sacred Heart of Jesus Camberwell London, a small group of people waited outside the modest church in anticipation of the young bride's arrival.

Tilly finally arrived with her proud father Ted in a hired model T Ford. Kate Wilson her oldest friend was the bridesmaid.

Jim had seconded Richard Hirsch, a mate in the army who was on leave at the time of the wedding, to be his best man.

The wedding certificate showed Tilly's age as twenty-five, but she was in fact sixteen.

After a very modest reception in the church hall, Jim and Tilly travelled to Blackpool by train. Jim had a further three days leave before returning to the 1st Australian Tunnelling Company.

They spent their time in bed with the odd fight thrown in; this is when Tilly received a black eye. This violence would continue for the remainder of their married life.

Jim returned to France and Tilly returned to the street with her husband's blessing.

Jim was missing his bride. It had been over a year since he had seen her, and the lovesick soldier decided it was time. He did not report for duty. Instead he caught a ship to London and lived in Camberwell for the next three months. The authorities caught up with him while he was having a drink at the local pub. He was arrested and incarcerated in the Lewes Detention Barracks East Sussex.

Lewis Detention Barracks

Jim was tried and given a three-month sentence and he forfeited 140 days' pay.

As far as the reluctant soldier was concerned gaol was better than being on the Western Front.

Workshop Where Jim Laboured

Jim Devine was released back to his unit on the Western Front where his welcome was less than enthusiastic. His comrades resented the six months he spent away from harm's way. Even if half his time was spent incarcerated at the Lewis Detention Centre they were more than aware the other half was spent having a good time with his wife.

The war was virtually over as the German High Command had accepted that Germany had been defeated. It took two more months of negotiation for the Armistice to be declared on the 11 November 1918.

Jim and the other diggers would soon be shipped home to Australia.

Tilly would follow soon after.

"All the News That's Fit to Print."

The New York Times.

THE WEATHER

NEW YORK, MONDAY, NOVEMBER 11, 1918.—TWENTY-FOUR PAGES.

VOL. LXVIII. NO. 21,984.

TWO CENTS

ARMISTICE SIGNED, END OF THE WAR!
BERLIN SEIZED BY REVOLUTIONISTS;
NEW CHANCELLOR BEGS FOR ORDER;
OUSTED KAISER FLEES TO HOLLAND

SON FLEES WITH EX-KAISER

Hindenburg Also Believed to be Among Those in His Party.

ALL ARE HEAVILY ARMED

Automobiles Bristle with Rifles as Fugitives Arrive at Dutch Frontier.

ON THEIR WAY TO DE STEEG

Belgians Yell to Them, "Are You On Your Way to Paris?"

LONDON, Nov. 10.—Both the former German Emperor and his eldest son, Frederick William, crossed the Dutch frontier Sunday morning, according to advices from The Hague. He reported continuation to De Steeg, near Utrecht.

Kaiser Fought Hindenburg's Call for Abdication; Failed to Get Army's Support in Keeping Throne

By GEORGE RENWICK

Copyright, 1918, by The New York Times Special Cable to The New York Times.

AMSTERDAM, Nov. 10.—

GERMAN DYNASTIES BEING WIPED OUT

King of Wurttemberg Abdicates—Sovereignty to Follow Suit.

PRINCES MAY BE EXILED

LONDON, Nov. 10.—A Havas dispatch from Basle says:

BERLIN TROOPS JOIN REVOLT

Reds Shell Building in Which Officers Vainly Resist.

THRONGS DEMAND REPUBLIC

Revolutionary Flag on Royal Palace — Crowd Packs Palace Also Seized.

GENERAL STRIKE IS BEGUN

Burgomaster and Police Submit—War Offices Now Under Socialist Control.

LONDON, Nov. 14.—

MORE WARSHIPS JOIN THE REDS

Four Dreadnoughts in Kiel Harbor Espouse the Revolutionary Cause.

GUARDSHIPS ALSO GO OVER

Those Protesting Mass in the Great Belt and the Baltic Abandon Their Posts.

LONDON, Nov. 10.—

Socialist Chancellor Appeals to All Germans To Help Him Save Fatherland from Anarchy

BERNE, Nov. 10. (Associated Press)—In an address to the people, the new German Chancellor, Friedrich Ebert, said:

COPENHAGEN, Nov. 10.—The new Berlin Government, according to a Wolff Bureau dispatch, has issued the following proclamation:

WAR ENDS AT 6 O'CLOCK THIS MORNING

The State Department in Washington Made the Announcement at 2:45 o'Clock.

ARMISTICE WAS SIGNED IN FRANCE AT MIDNIGHT

Terms Include Withdrawal from Alsace-Lorraine, Disarming and Demobilization of Army and Navy, and Occupation of Strategic Naval and Military Points.

By The Associated Press.

WASHINGTON, Monday, Nov. 11, 2:48 A. M.—The armistice between Germany, on the one hand, and the allied Governments and the United States, on the other, has been signed.

The State Department announced at 2:45 o'clock this morning that Germany had signed.

The department's announcement simply said: "The armistice has been signed."

The world war will end this morning at 6 o'clock, Washington time, 11 o'clock Paris time. The armistice was signed by the German representatives at midnight.

This announcement was made by the State Department at 2:50 o'clock this morning.

The terms of the armistice, it was announced, will not be made public until later. Military men here, however, regard it as certain that they include:

Immediate retirement of the German military forces from France, Belgium, and Alsace-Lorraine.

Disarming and demobilization of the German armies.

Occupation by the allied and American forces of such strategic points in Germany as will make impossible a renewal of hostilities.

Delivery of part of the German High Seas Fleet and a certain number of submarines to the allied and American naval forces.

Disarmament of all other German warships

WELCOME TO
STEAK & KIDNEY
TILLY

CHAPTER 6

After the war ended, Jim and Tilly had two children; a girl who died at birth and a boy they named Frederick.

Jim was shipped back to Sydney on the troop ship *Karoola*.

Tilly continued her career as a prostitute, using the same corner close to the Strand Hotel for another twelve months until setting sail on the *Waimana*, a bride ship transporting English brides to Australia to reunite with their Australian husbands.

Frederick didn't accompany her, as he was adopted by Tilly's parents. Tilly would never see her son again.

After six weeks of seasickness and boredom, Tilly arrived at Circular Quay, to be met by Jim.

Once their greetings were concluded Jim took his bride back to his rented flat in Paddington.

'Jim, I thought we were going to your kangaroo farm, not this little shit box. What the fuck is going on?'

'Oh, come on Tilly you didn't really believe I owned a fucking kangaroo farm, did you?'

'You told me you did.'

'It was just a bit of a joke. I thought you'd realise it.'

'No, I didn't realise it, you arse hole.'

'Sorry Tilly.'

'So, what do you expect me to do now?'

'Go back on the job, love, do what you're best at.'

'So what in the fuck are you going to do, Jim?'

'I'll be your pimp, babe... plus I'm sure I'll be able to rustle up some dosh here and there, you know me.'

Tilly did her research and she discovered Eastern Sydney was the place to practise her profession. This red-light district had been popular for many years. Tilly was very popular with the patrons and as a result, together with Jim's illegal pursuits, they began accumulating wealth.

The young Englishwoman with her peaches and cream complexion and blonde hair became one of the best-known prostitutes in Darlinghurst and Paddington. She had a reputation of being a generous soul. Anyone that approached her with a tale of woe would be supported by her.

After a night's work, Tilly would return to the flat where she and Jim would count the night's earnings on the kitchen table.

If things became a little quiet Tilly would gravitate to Woolloomooloo or Kings Cross.

On one particular morning about 3 am, the Devines arrived home after a night of cavorting in Kings Cross.

'Hey Tilly, look what I got today, love.'

'What's that, darl?'

Jim held out his left forearm, rolling up his shirtsleeve to display his new tattoo.

Tilly.

'Jim, that's lovely. I'm too tired to fuck you, babe, but I'll give you a suck.'

A Street in Woolloomooloo

William Street, 1916.

Approaching Kings Cross

Tilly was standing on the corner of Palmer and Liverpool Streets waiting for her next client when a plain-clothes policeman approached her.

'Hello darling, how much?'

'For a handsome chap like you ten shillings.'

'Right well, you're nicked, sweetheart. You'll have to come with me.'

Sergeant Burgess clasped handcuffs onto the pretty young blonde and escorted her to Darlinghurst Police Station where she was charged with whoring. She was also charged with obscene language, having called the policeman 'a fucking flat-footed prick'.

These occurrences became more frequent. Between 1921 and 1925 Tilly was arrested and charged no fewer than seventy-nine times for whoring, offensive behaviour, obscene language and assault. Most of these charges brought a fine or a few days in gaol, but that all changed when she met Frank Wilcox, a commercial traveller, on January 11th, 1925.

Tilly was standing at her favourite corner in Palmer Street when a man in a grey suit approached her.

'Hello darling, don't you look smart tonight,' Tilly said.

'Well, thank you! You look pretty good yourself, sweetheart.'

'So, I take it you're looking for a good time?'

'That's right. How much will it cost me?'

'That depends on how long you want me and what you'd like me to do.'

'I'd like the best you've got, darling.'

'All right, that'll set you back £5.'

'That's a lot of dosh but I'm sure you're worth it. Where do we go?'

'Take my hand and I'll lead you to bliss.'

Tilly had a private room she rented close by.

The pair entered the room Tilly immediately began undressing her client. Once naked, she led him to the bed. She undressed slowly. teasing him as she did so.

She joined him on the bed, laid him down and took him in her mouth. She sucked him until he came in her mouth.

'Good boy. Now that you've got rid of your load we can take our time.'

Tilly demonstrated all of her skills over the next hour until Frank was exhausted.

'How did you enjoy that, Frank?'

'Bloody good, Tilly, but I have a confession to make.'

'You haven't got the clap, have you?'

'No, I'm clean as a whistle.'

'So what is it, love?'

I only have £2 in my wallet.'

'What, you bastard, you ripped me off I should have got your money up front.'

Tilly kept a nightstick in the bedside drawer given to her by Jim who stole it from a policeman. She kept it so she could protect herself if she was attacked.

She grabbed it and beat the travelling salesman to within an inch of his life, leaving him on the floor in a pool of blood.

The police arrived at Tilly and Jim's flat the next morning and took her away.

Tilly went to trial, was found guilty and sentenced to six months at Long Bay Gaol.

She soon made it known to the rest of the inmates that although she was only twenty-five she was a woman not to be messed with despite her nickname "Pretty Tilly".

Once Tilly was released, the young married couple continued on their wayward lifestyle. Jim too was constantly interned in Long Bay for various offences including assault and larceny. This was no normal marriage.

FEBRUARY 1925

One afternoon Tilly was sitting at the kitchen table drinking a cup of tea when Jim burst in holding his face; blood was oozing out between his fingers.

'What the fuck happened to you, Jim? Who did this to you?'

'Never mind who fucking slashed me, Till, just stich me up.'

'I want to know who did this.'

'Till, I'm bleeding to death, love. Just stich me up.'

Tilly went to the drawer in the kitchen hutch and removed a large needle and thread.

'Take your hand away, darl. I need to see what I'm doing. Shit there's blood everywhere. Hold on, Jim. I'll get a face washer to clean it up.'

Tilly wiped the cut with the warm face washer and began to stich the wound, all the while wiping the blood away allowing her to see what she was doing. Finally she finished the final stich; number thirty-two. Jim would be scarred for life.

'You lie down for a while, love and take it easy. I've just got to pop out for a little while.'

Tilly had a very good idea who had slashed her husband and she went looking for him with a razor in her handbag. As she passed the barbershop in Liverpool Street she peered in through the large plate window where she saw the culprit sitting in the barber's chair getting a shave.

I'll give him a fucking shave all right, she thought.

She entered the shop, screaming at the top of her voice.

'You fucking prick, you cut my Jim! Well now it's your turn you bastard.'

Tilly pulled out the razor and slashed Sam Wilson across the face from just below his right eye down to his lip. The patrons waiting for the barber's services grabbed the enraged woman while one of them ran to find a policeman.

Tilly went to trial, was found guilty of grievous bodily harm and sentenced to two years in Long Bay Gaol.

Jim received a sentence of eighteen months for living off the immoral earnings of a prostitute; namely Tilly.

It was during this stay at Her Majesty's pleasure that Tilly decided it was high time to give the game away. She decided to open a brothel and hire girls to do the hard work.

RED LIGHTS

CHAPTER 7

1927

Tilly and Big Jim were released from Long Bay about the same time.

They celebrated their respective releases at their favourite restaurant *Bonne Femme* in Palmer Street, Darlinghurst.

'Jim, I decided while I was in the Bay that I would no longer lie on my back to earn a living.'

'Come on Till; you earn bloody good money being a whore. What do you intend to do? Become a fucking seamstress or something?'

'Settle down, love. I didn't say I was leaving the profession. What I'm saying is I am going to open a brothel and employ others to do the work while you and I count the money.'

'Don't you think it would be difficult to rent premises? Not many landlords would agree to rent out to a brothel.'

'I agree so it's my intention to purchase a suitable building. I've been saving since I arrived in Sydney.'

'Good on you, love.'

'Yeah well after over ten years in the game I figure it's time for a change.'

Tilly began her search for a suitable house in the right area. She found one in Palmer Street just near William Street where she knew the area well.

The next step was to fit it out. The first priority was double beds, and she decorated each room with French style décor.

The waiting room was fitted with velvet lounges, and Tiffany lamps. A gramophone was also provided.

The final step was a red light in the window, and she was now ready for business. Tilly exploited the law that stated it was illegal for a male to operate a brothel but not so for a woman.

Tilly recruited girls she knew from the street to work for her.

Tilly's girls paid a percentage to Tilly; generally twenty-five percent. The girls got to use the brothel's facilities and were protected from any imminent danger they may encounter in the street.

There wasn't a typical Tilly girl; some were seasoned prostitutes while others were housewives trying to make ends meet.

The brothel was profitable from day one. Tilly soon opened another in Chapel Street and nine months later another in Woods Lane and soon after one in Berwick Lane; all within a few square miles of each other.

Tilly could walk to all her premises, as they were all located in the same area where she and Jim lived.

She made it her business to be available to her girls. If they had a problem or were finding it difficult to get by the madam would lend them money, so she was regarded as a kind soul. However, if one of her girls tried to steal from her she was sacked and quite often beaten.

COCAINE

Jim approached his wife with a new scheme; he proposed that instead of paying the girls their share with cold hard cash they pay them in cocaine. The girls could either use the drug or sell it on the streets or to their clients at a tidy profit.

'Can't you see the benefit, Tilly? We buy the dope in bulk, package it and pay the girls. Our percentage should increase from twenty-five to forty or so. We'll be laughing.'

'Do you reckon the girls will be happy with the deal, Jim?'

'If they don't like it they can fuck off and we recruit girls that are happy with the arrangement.

'We get them hooked on the stuff and they aren't going to leave us. It's a loyalty thing.'

'All right darl, let's give it a go for a while.'

Jim purchased the drug from his underworld contacts and Tilly convinced her girls it was a great deal. Only a few of her older girls baulked and decided to leave.

After twelve months Tilly and Jim had accumulated enough money to purchase several more houses in Darlinghurst and Woolloomooloo. They now had eighteen very profitable brothels.

Tilly returned home after a busy day managing her sex empire to find Jim drinking a beer in the lounge room.

'Hello sweetheart, how was your day?'

'Good, apart from the usual stuff I put up with. I looked at a house in Maroubra today.'

'Geez Tilly I don't think a bordello in Maroubra is such a flash idea; it's a bit posh don't you think?'

'I wasn't looking at it for business. I thought it would be nice for us to live in.'

'Bloody hell— how much are they asking?'

'Just £1700.'

'So you reckon we can afford a place like that?'

'I do, in fact, I bought it.'

'You didn't.'

'I fucking did; we take possession in two months.'

'There's no doubt about you, girl, you're a mover and a shaker.'

Maroubra Home

Torrington Street was never the same again. Their neighbours were horrified; if it wasn't loud riotous parties to all hours of the morning it was Tilly and Jim fighting. The police were also regular visitors to the Maroubra bungalow. More often than not they would find Tilly with a black eye or other injuries, but she didn't press charges. Nor did she ever during her turbulent marriage to Jim.

Apart from the violence, Tilly and Jim were enjoying a good life. Tilly's brothels continued to be profitable, and Jim established himself as one of the major players in the drug trade.

The only fly in the ointment for Tilly was her arch-rival, Kate Leigh.

KISS ME KATE

Kate Leigh was born on March 10, 1881, in Dubbo New South Wales as the eighth child of Timothy Beahan, a boot maker, and his wife Charlotte.

Dubbo 1881

'Have you seen that little bitch of a daughter lately, Charlotte?'

'No Tim, what's she done now?'

'I left some change on the kitchen dresser this morning and now it's gone. I'm sure she stole it.'

'Well, you'll have to confront her when she gets home from school.'

'That's if the little bitch went to school; she's always wagging it.'

'Don't be too hard on her, Tim. She's just a kid.'

'I don't care, love, she needs a bloody good lesson and that's what she'll get.'

They both heard the front door open.

Kate sneaked into her bedroom, which she shared with her three sisters.

'Kate is that you? Come into the kitchen. I want to talk to you,' her father yelled.

'What do you want?'

'What I want is an explanation of where my money disappeared to,' said Tim.

'I don't know what you're talking about.'

'Where's your purse?'

'I lost it.'

'Don't lie to me you, little bitch. I know you took my money.'

The angry father took off his belt, grabbed his daughter, laid her over his knee and whipped her as hard as he could. By the time he'd finished her buttocks were bleeding. Kate ran to her room crying.

The next morning Kate was nowhere to be seen. She didn't join the family for breakfast and nor did she return for dinner. It became obvious Kate had run away from home. She returned a week later, and her mother insisted her husband not beat her for her indiscretion.

This was not the first time Kate was beaten or ran away from home and nor would it be the last; eventually she was sent to the Parramatta Industrial School for Girls, a very draconian establishment where schooling was minimal and forced labour was the first priority.

For the next four years Kate was trained in domestic service duties. She became proficient in laundering, kitchen duties, and cleaning.

Finally she was released and headed to Sydney where she found work in various factories and shops around Glebe and Surrey Hills.

Kate began to mix with unsavoury types around Surrey Hills, a very rough area. Her first arrest and internment occurred when she turned twenty on a charge of vagrancy.

On her release from gaol she met Jack Leigh, a carpenter who was ten years her senior. After a short courtship they married on May 2nd, 1902.

Kate produced a daughter, Eileen, soon after.

Although Jack described himself as a carpenter he earned his money from illegal bookmaking and larceny.

AUGUST 1902

Jack was involved in an incident that would change both his and Kate's lives.

Jack was home in the couple's rented flat in Glebe when there was a loud knock on the door.

'Who is it?' he yelled.

'Harry Bryson. I'm here to collect your rent.'

'Fuck off; it's not due until Saturday.'

'I need to collect it today.'

Jack jumped up from his chair and opened the door.

'I'm not paying you a fucking penny until Saturday so you can just fuck off, you little turd.'

'I need to collect it today. I'm going to Bathurst to see my sick mother.'

'I don't give a flying fuck about your mother. I'm not paying you until it's due.'

'I don't like your attitude, Mr Leigh.'

'Don't you? Well how do you like this?'

Jack hit Harry square on the nose, breaking it. He then continued to bash the rent collector to within an inch of his life and left him lying in a pool of blood outside his front door.

Jack's neighbour heard the commotion and investigated. He immediately called the police who arrived within twenty minutes. Harry Bryson was taken to hospital where he stayed for two weeks.

The police arrested Jack and charged him assault with intent to kill. Kate returned home to the Glebe flat only to find Jack drinking a bottle of whisky and lamenting his bad luck.

Kate promised her husband she would concoct a watertight alibi, which would get him off the charge.

Jack faced court the following week. Kate was in attendance ready to deliver her testimony.

Eventually she was called to the witness stand.

Jack's Barrister, Allan Willing. addressed the young woman.

'Please state your name, madam.'

'Kate Leigh.'

'What is your relationship to the defendant?'

'He's my husband.'

'Can you tell the court in your own words what happened on August 10th, 1902, in your Glebe flat?'

'Mr Bryson the landlord knocked on the door demanding our rent. The rent was due, but we didn't have the money to pay.

'Mr Bryson was very angry, threatening to evict us immediately. He then suggested if I slept with him, he would forego a week's rent.'

'So, did you sleep with Mr Bryson, Mrs Leigh?'

'I felt I had no choice.'

'What happened next?'

'Jack came home and caught us in bed together. He went into a rage, beating Mr Bryson and throwing him out into the corridor.'

'So you believe your husband had every right to bash Mr Bryson?'

'I do; he was defending my honour.'

The jury didn't buy Kate's story and both she and Jack were sentenced to five years in Long Bay Gaol. She was charged with corroboration and perjury.

They were both released around the same time and immediately separated.

Kate was able to rent a one-bedroom flat in Glebe and she was given custody of her daughter Eileen. She found employment in a shoe factory where she cut the leather ready for the cordwainers.

The pay was meagre, and Kate found it difficult to pay her rent and care for her daughter. The young Kate was quite attractive with a curvy figure, and she decided to use these assets by becoming a prostitute part-time in and around Kings Cross.

It was during this period she met her arch-rival Tilly Devine. From their first meeting, they despised each other. She resigned from the shoe company and became a full-time criminal, continuing as a whore but also stealing and selling alibis to known criminals facing charges in court.

1922

Kate divorced Jack since they hadn't lived together for some years and she soon married another petty criminal, Teddy Barry—a musician from Western Australia. Kate continued her criminal career, as did Teddy.

NOVEMBER 4, 1922

Kate decided to finish her shift in Kings Cross early, as she was feeling unwell. She arrived at her Glebe flat at 10 pm only to find Teddy in bed with another woman. Kate fell into a rage. She grabbed a cricket bat that was kept in the corner of the bedroom for protection and laid into the naked couple, beating them senseless.

'Now get out the both of you! I don't want to see either of you again,' she stormed when Teddy woke up.

'It's not what it looks like, babe,' said Teddy.

'Really? You were chocker block up her when I walked in. What am I meant to think? Now get the fuck out, you bastard.'

Once Teddy had vacated the premises. Kate began a series of relationships with a number of small-time crooks.

One of Kate's lovers was Jewey Freeman. They lived together in the notorious Frog Hollow in Sydney's inner west.

Jewey Freeman

Frog Hollow

It was in the Frog Hollow terrace that an infamous plan to rob the payroll of Eveleigh Railway was hatched.

THE PAYROLL HEIST

It was the morning of 10 June 1914, payday at the Eveleigh Railway Workshops on Wilson Street, Sydney, when the robbery took place. Paymaster for the NSW Railways, Frederick Charles Miller, along with his junior, John Henry, arrived at the factory complex in a horse-drawn wagon. Albert Andrews was driving the wagon that day, as he had on many occasions. They were returning from the bank with two cash boxes on the tray: one containing £3696; the other, £3302.

'We had just pulled up when two men, including Norman Twiss, met us. The first strong box was taken into the office ready to be distributed to the workers. They returned to us to take the second box when I saw a car scream up skidding to a halt,' said Miller.

The car was driven by Ernie Ryan commonly called Shiner, with Jewey Freeman in the passenger seat. Both men were wearing bandanna masks and driving goggles.

'The bloke who was the passenger jumped out of the car shouting, "this is a bail up". He had a pistol, which he pointed at my head. He pushed me to the ground and told me to keep my head down or he'd blow it off. He ordered Twiss to hand over the cash box which he did very carefully,' said Miller.

Robert Hodge, one of the men who met the horses and dray, tried to retrieve one of the boxes but he was told to move away, or he would be shot.

The two gangsters drove away at high speed with the moneyboxes in the back seat.

A bystander observing the robbery took down the licence plate of the getaway car. The police traced it back to a mechanic who had reported the car stolen the previous day.

A reward of £400 was offered.

NEW SOUTH WALES

POLICE   GAZETTE,

AND WEEKLY RECORD OF CRIME.

No. 24.]   WEDNESDAY, 17 JUNE.   [1914.

NOTICE.

For Instructions as to Reports for Compilation of Police Gazette, vide No. 1 of this year.

NOTICE.

APPOINTMENT VACANT.

Cumnock—*North-eastern District*—Carrying the rank and pay of Sergeant, Second Class (Mounted), Electoral Registrar, Crown Lands Bailiff, and other usual extraneous appointments.

Applications from Police considering themselves entitled to this position may be made by telegram through the Superintendent, who will append his remarks thereon.

A decision will be arrived at on the 1st proximo.

ERNEST C. DAY,
Inspector-General of Police.

[Extracts from the Government Gazette.]

[9185]   Chief Secretary's Office,
Sydney, 17th June, 1914.

ROBBERY UNDER ARMS.—£400 REWARD.

WHEREAS on or about noon on the 10th instant, a cash-box containing the sum of £3,301 in notes, gold, and silver, the property of the Chief Commissioner for Railways of New South Wales, was stolen from Mr. Frederick Charles Miller, Railway Paymaster, at Wilson-street, Newtown, near the entrance to Eveleigh Work-sheds, by two masked and armed offenders, who absconded in a motor-car. Notice is hereby given that a reward of Four Hundred Pounds will be paid by Government for such information as shall lead to the apprehension and conviction of the said two armed offenders, or the sum of Two Hundred Pounds will be paid for such information as shall lead to the apprehension and conviction of either one of them; also a further sum of ten per cent. will be paid on any amount of the stolen money that may be recovered. In addition to the above reward, His Excellency the Governor will be advised to extend a free pardon to any accomplice, not being one of the two armed offenders, who shall first give such required information. This reward to remain in force for three months only.

J. H. CANN.

A warrant has now been issued by the Redfern Bench for the arrest of two men whose names are unknown, but who can be identified, and whose descriptions are as follows, charged that on the tenth day of June, 1914, at Redfern, being armed with an offensive weapon, to wit, a revolver, in company together did rob Frederick Charles Miller of the sum of three thousand three hundred and one pounds, the property of the Chief Commissioner for Railways and Tramways, such being an offence punishable on indictment in the State of New South Wales.—First.—30 years of age, short, strongly built, clean shaved, wearing a yellow overcoat or motor coat, collar of which was turned up hiding ears and part of face, wearing motor goggles, larger than ordinary motor goggles, also wearing long skirted, well-cut, grey sac suit. Second.—35 years of age, much bigger than man previously described; wearing dark motor cap and goggles. Special inquiry is directed to be made as to the whereabouts of Henry Lewis, alias James McKay, alias Samuel Freeman, alias Frederick Wilson, alias Morris, alias "Jonsey," whose description is 30 years of age, 5 feet 5½ inches high (without boots), dark-brown hair, brown eyes, Australian flag, sailor's head and flower on inside left forearm, female's bust and flower on inside right forearm, mole on right upper lip, and scar on left chin, and whose photograph is published hereunder as he is believed to be one of the two armed offenders; see also New South Wales Photo. Book 44, page 116 as Samuel Freeman, and West Australian Photo. Register, number 347 C. (the latter as James McKay).

May be accompanied by Maud Wilson, alias Ryan, alias Jones, alias Halford, 31 years of age, 5 feet 6

The thieves' plan was to travel to Melbourne and then on to the United States. With so much money involved the gang had planned to lay low for a while or so you would think.

Shiner Ryan

Shiner took his girl out the night before the robbery, telling her he would be rich very soon.

After the robbery, he arranged to see her again.

'Hello, Ettie. I told you I'd be rich. Here's £100, darling; go and buy some new clothes.'

'Thank you, honey. Come here and I'll thank you the way I know you like it.'

When undressing her lover she noticed he was wearing a new diamond ring and the pockets of his trousers were stuffed with pound notes and a revolver.

The next morning after breakfast Shiner announced he was going to take Ettie into the city and buy her a present.

The couple caught the tram into the city centre where Shiner and Ettie entered Solomon's Jewellery store. He bought her two gold bangles and a diamond ring. He purchased a gold watch for himself.

Over the next few weeks, expensive dinners were consumed accompanied by French champagne. Shiner and Ettie was living the good life.

Ryan decided to send the remainder of the loot to Melbourne where he had arranged for his good mate Sam Faulkiner to hold onto it for him until he arrived.

When Ryan arrived in Melbourne he discovered that Faulkiner had absconded with the money, not to the USA, but to Tasmania.

His bad luck continued. He was arrested in Melbourne. The police found £600 of the payroll hidden in a glass jar up the chimney of the house he was renting in Collingwood. This stash was the only money recovered from the Eveleigh robbery.

Jewey Freeman was arrested on June 24th, about to board a train to Melbourne. His alibi was he had been at the horse races on the day of the robbery. The police were sceptical, arresting him for armed robbery and assault.

As the investigation continued the police became convinced both Twiss and Tatham, the getaway car's owner, were members of the gang.

A railway worker who had known Twiss for some time told police Twiss had mentioned to him how easy it would be to rob the payroll.

A barmaid at Flanagan's Hotel reported she had seen Jewey and Twiss together several times prior to the crime, including the day of the actual robbery. She had also seen Tatham with them.

Both Twiss and Tatham were arrested on June 11 and charged with armed robbery and assault.

CENTRAL CRIMINAL COURT – DARLINGHURST
JULY 23, 1914

The gang of four, Freeman, Ryan, Twiss and Tatham all pleaded not guilty to the charges of assault and stealing £3302.

Freeman also faced a charge of shooting and wounding Michael McHale, a night watchman who foiled him from robbing the Paddington Post Office days before the Eveleigh robbery.

Twiss was acquitted due to lack of evidence against him.

Shiner concocted an elaborate story, telling the court he was an inventor who was in Sydney only to find investors for his inventions. He was adamant he was not guilty, but the court thought differently and sentenced Shiner to ten years in Parramatta Gaol.

He didn't settle into prison life. Initially he attempted suicide by slashing his wrists. He was unsuccessful in his attempt and finally settled in. He wrote to Ettie on a regular basis throughout his term.

Jewey Freeman had the most serious charges against him; his girlfriend Kate Leigh, known for providing false alibis, came to his defence.

She told the court she and Jewey were skating at the Exhibition Skating Rink on June 5th and then returned together to Miss Leigh's house the following afternoon.

Her alibi came unstuck when Ettie Kelly and May Bragg told the court they were with Jewey Freeman the night of the 5th of June.

It was also noted that the skating rink was closed at the time Kate was meant to be skating with Freeman.

Another criminal was staying at Kate Leigh's house at the time of the robbery. Leigh attempted to force Raymond Moore into testifying he had seen Jewey at Kate's house on the day of the robbery.

He refused to commit perjury; consequently, Kate retrieved a tomahawk from the backyard and hit her houseguest, breaking his arm.

The court refuted Leigh's testimony. charging her with perjury. She was sentenced to seven years gaol, which was considered harsh. Freeman was sentenced to ten years gaol.

Freeman was used to prison life, but never really coped all that well.

Kate on the other hand soon established herself as number one bitch. She controlled the illicit drug trade. All the prisoners knew not to cross Kate Leigh, or she would set one of her gang around to bash you.

Despite her illegal activities Kate was seen to conform to the prison regulations by the prison guards; she was required to exercise and endure cold showers winter and summer. She worked in the kitchen preparing meals for the prison population.

Kate was also a regular visitor to the prison chapel, praying daily.

The authorities were obviously impressed with her behaviour for she was released from Long Bay two years early.

Kate had been incarcerated for the duration of the Great War. While she was languishing in Parramatta Gaol close to thirty-five million people lost their lives. Another fifty to one hundred million had died from the Spanish Flu. The young woman had got off rather well, considering.

Kate was freed at a very opportune time; temperance organisations had been lobbying the Government to introduce 6 pm closing as a means of reducing alcohol consumption and ensuring the menfolk returned home at a reasonable hour. The law passed; no longer could pubs stay open until 11 pm.

Kate established a series of sly-grog shops, places where both men and women could enjoy a beer, wine or spirit after hours.

Within a reasonably short period of time, she was able to purchase a terrace home in East Sydney where she and Eileen lived. Sly-grog was the pillar of Kate's criminal empire.

Kate and Teddy Giving Out Christmas Presents
From the balcony of her Surrey Hills terrace

Mum's the Word

Kate established a network of hotels and liquor suppliers who were willing to take the risk to supply her with grog for her establishments.

The next step in building her new career was to rent six premises to house her sly-grog shops. Some were salubrious, attracting the upper end of the social spectrum. Others were blood houses frequented by gangsters and whores. The password for all of them was *Mum's in*.

Sam Wilson and his wife Vida had been to the Tivoli Theatre to see *Maid of the Mountains*, a bright and light musical they both enjoyed.

'I don't particularly want to go home yet, Sam.'

'Well, darling, we could go to a café for a coffee if you like.'

'No, that's boring. Let's go and have a drink at Kate's place. I believe it's very nice.'

'Do you know where it is darling?'

'Yes, Susan told me where it was the other day.'

The young couple hailed a taxi and instructed the driver to take them to 212 Devonshire Street Surry Hills.

'Certainly, so you feel like a tipple at Kate's sly-grog establishment?'

'So you know about it do you, driver?'

'Everybody knows Kate's places; even the cops. I was in there once and recognised the Chief Magistrate.'

'Well that makes me feel safe from the law,' said Vida.

The taxi pulled up outside a large terrace house painted white.

'Right, this is it, the finest of Kate Leigh's sly-grog establishments. That'd be two shillings thank you.'

Sam paid the taxi driver and helped Vida out of the car. They approached the red front door and knocked twice. After a few minutes, the door was opened by no other than Kate Leigh herself.

'Hello, you two; what's the password?'

'Mum's in.'

'That's it. Come on in and make yourselves comfortable. Now, what can I get you to drink?'

Sam ordered a glass of whisky. Vida asked for a glass of champagne.

Once they received their drinks, having paid top price for the privilege, they sat down on Chesterfield lounge. Vida and Sam were very impressed with the décor overall. It created a warm atmosphere.

As the couple was enjoying their second glass, a thunderous banging on the front door could be heard.

'Open up. This is a police raid.'

Kate came into the main room mumbling, 'fucking cops, I pay them enough to leave me alone.'

The Queen of sly-grog opened the door and found six policemen, batons in hand.

'My name is Sergeant Brumby. I have reason to believe you are selling alcohol illegally after closing time.'

'Come on, Daniel, you know I do; you drink here yourself as do half the cops you have standing behind you.'

'I am required by law to close down the premises and arrest you. The patrons currently here need to vacate the premises immediately.'

'Here we fucking go again.'

Kate was arrested and subsequently convicted, serving a seven-day gaol term at Long Bay.

A short gaol term didn't worry Kate. It gave her a break from owning and operating twenty sly groggeries.

During her illustrious career, Kate served thirteen gaol terms and received 107 criminal convictions.

Kate was making a fortune with her sly-grog shops, but it wasn't enough. She could see how much her arch-rival, Tilly Devine, was making running her brothels. Kate decided to go into opposition with Tilly, running several brothels in roughly the same area as her nemesis.

The war was about to begin.

Kate had assembled a gang of gangsters and thugs to protect her business. They would also protect her newly established brothels and cocaine businesses.

Kate, Eileen and Gang

Kate knew it was essential for her to find the right premises to house her brothels. Her first red light was displayed in the window of 69 Devonshire Street the same street she and Eileen resided. The second and third opened soon after; one in Woolloomooloo the other in Palmer Street Darlinghurst. She had now infringed on Tilly Devine's territory.

Kate also knew it was essential to gather the right staff to work in her bordellos. She went out onto the streets in search of the right girls. When she found one she thought was suitable, she would approach her in a warm and friendly manner, promising her better working conditions and a higher share of the fee. Kate didn't care if the new recruit was independent or was part of Tilly Devine's stable.

Kate had ventured out onto the streets of Darlinghurst in the company of two of her thugs, Stretch Hailes and Oogie Irvine when she spotted a petite redhead standing on the corner of Palmer Street and Kings Lane.

'Hello darling, how's business?'

'The answer to that question depends on who's asking, love?'

'My name is Kate Leigh. You may have heard of me.'

'Yeah, I've heard of you. My pimp, Jim Devine, speaks of you in glowing terms.'

'I bet he fucking does. He and his lovely wife Tilly and I don't get on all that well.'

'So, you asked me how's business. It's okay. I've had better.'

'Could I interest you in working in one of my luxurious establishments?'

'Maybe, but what's the benefit to me?'

'Well, it means you are off the streets, and you're protected by bodyguards like Dave and Oogie here. No chance of being beaten up by rough clients. The working conditions are clean and comfortable and not only that, but I guarantee you will earn more than you do at the moment.'

'I must admit it sounds tempting.'

'I tell you what love… actually what is your name?'

'Annie.'

'Well, Annie, why don't you come back with me, and I will show you around?'

'I suppose it wouldn't hurt, although if Jim Devine finds out about it he'll slash me across my pretty face.'

'You needn't worry about Big Jim, Annie. My boys will take care of him.'

Kate and the boys escorted Annie to the Devonshire brothel where Kate introduced her to the other girls waiting in the lounge.

'Kate, I'm impressed. You have done yourself proud.'

'Thank you, Annie. So you can see yourself working here?'

'I can. When can I start?'

'You can get started whenever it suits you, darling.'

'How about tomorrow night? I'll need to purchase some fancy clothes to fit in here. I'll go into the city tomorrow.'

'That sounds fair enough, but do you have enough money? I can lend you some.'

'Actually, I could use some more. I had to pay the rent today.'

'I understand. Here, take ten quid; that should buy you some nice glad rags.'

'Thank you, Kate, I appreciate it.'

'Nothing too glamorous, mind you, we can't have you showing up the other girls.'

'I don't think there's too much chance of doing that.'

'So Annie, we'll see you tomorrow say 9 pm okay?'

'I'm looking forward to it, Kate.'

Kate was concerned. The designated 9 pm came and went. It was now midnight and her new girl had not shown up.

I hope she's all right. She's got ten quid of my money as well, Kate thought.

Annie wasn't all right. Jim Device had got wind of her plans to join up with Kate. He paid her a visit at her Redfern terrace, confronting her with the accusation she was deserting Tilly's stable. He beat her so severely she was taken to a hospital where she stayed for a week.

When Kate heard what had happened to her star recruit she organised Oogie and Stretch to pay Jim Devine a visit. They found him at the bar of the *Tradesmen's Arms*. They grabbed him and dragged him out into the laneway at the back of the hotel and gave him a beating he would never forget. Strangely they didn't use their cutthroat razors on their adversary.

Altercations between Tilly's and Kate's gangs became a common occurrence.

Razors became the weapon of choice after the Government introduced the *Pistol Licensing Act* of 1927. Any person caught with an unlicensed firearm received an automatic prison sentence. The gangsters reverted to cutthroat razors.

Tilly's gang all carried finely sharpened razors on their person, as did Kate's. Although there were deaths caused by a razor attack, more often than not they were used to intimidate and slash, leaving a scar across the victim's face for the rest of their lives. Male or female, it didn't matter to the gangsters.

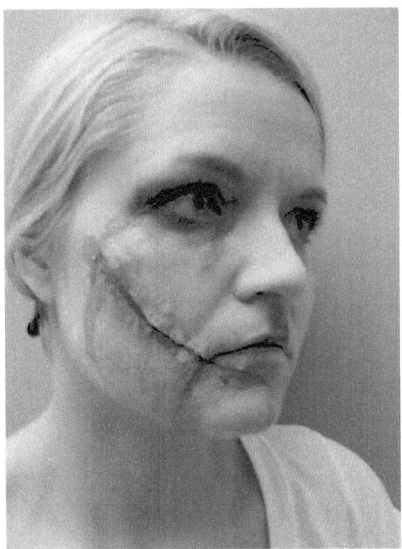

THE RAZOR WINS

CHAPTER 11

1929

Eileen Leigh turned out to be a chip off the old block; she followed her mother Kate into a life of crime working in Kate's organisation as a loyal deputy.

Eileen had taken up with another member of the Leigh gang, William Smiley, a handsome debonair thug who would slash an adversary without hesitation.

Eileen had got wind that a local barber William Darby Lloyd was selling cocaine to traditional Leigh customers, undercutting their price per ounce significantly. His partner in crime was William Scott, a swarthy little criminal who was known to have got his own sister hooked on snow.

Eileen instructed Smiley to find the bastards and teach them a lesson.

The couple went out looking for the barber and his sidekick in the streets of Darlinghurst. As they turned into Liverpool Street from Palmer Street, Eileen spotted them.

'Smiley, there they are! Get the bastards.'

The gangster ran up to the pair who was walking in the opposite direction, hitting both over the back of the head with a steel pipe. They both dropped to the footpath, stunned.

'Right you bastards, this will teach you both to undersell Kate and Eileen Leigh.'

Smiley produced a razor, slashing both their faces several times.

By the time the police found them they were near death, bleeding profusely. Blood was running down the gutter of Liverpool Street.

To finish them off, Eileen kicked both of them in the groin.

Lloyd and Scott were treated at St Vincent's Hospital where Lloyd received sixty stitches, and Scott, fifty.

An eyewitness, Sydney York, called the police, and he also testified when Smiley faced the court.

When Smiley was arrested, Kate Leigh posted the £400 bail.

As usual in the criminal world, Lloyd and Scott testified that it wasn't Smiley who perpetrated the crime but an unrecognised attacker.

Sydney York was called and recounted exactly what he had seen in Liverpool Street.

The judge believed York, not Lloyd and Scott, and he sent Smiley away for five years in Long Bay Gaol.

Sydney York soon realised his life was in danger and moved to Melbourne.

Smiley was released from gaol in 1932, re-joining Kate Leigh's razor gang. However his freedom was short lived as he was shot by an unknown assailant and left to die in a Surry Hills street. No one was charged with his murder.

MELBOURNE 1915

Norman Bruhn came from a traditional Geelong clan and his family had been on the wrong side of the law for generations.

He had grown up with a fascination for guns. It was this fascination that enticed him to join the Geelong-based company of the 70th Infantry, which was part of the 18th Infantry Brigade headquartered at Ballarat. This was one of the many civilian militias, Commonwealth-funded and equipped, that was set up to defend Australia if it was ever invaded. It was an army of volunteers, often drawn from local rifle clubs. This experience put the apprentice gangster in a good position to enlist when war broke out.

In 1914, war broke out between Germany and her allies and Great Britain and hers.

Young Norman enlisted. Having spent fourteen days in gaol for offensive behaviour he thought it would be for the best to stay off the streets.

Attached to the AIF's 6th Battalion, Norman embarked for active service on 2nd of February 1915, shipping out from Port Melbourne on the *Clan MacGillivray*, a converted merchant ship.

The majority of the 6th Battalion had landed in Egypt before Norman had enlisted and had been well and truly ensconced in Mena Camp marching in scorching heat and taking part in activities such as camel riding and climbing the pyramids.

The 6th Battalion was part of the 2nd Australian Infantry Brigade. They would participate in the second wave of the landing at Anzac Cove on 25th of April 1915. Norman, however, was in the battalion's 2nd Reinforcements and did not arrive at Gallipoli until mid-May.

Norman's luck was running his way. He not only missed the landing at Anzac Cove but also the Second Battle of Krithia.

THE SECOND BATTLE OF KRITHIA

After the first attempt to capture the village of Krithia, on the Gallipoli Peninsula, failed on April 28, 1915, a second was initiated on May 6th by Allied troops under the British commander Sir Aylmer Hunter-Weston.

Fortified by 105 pieces of heavy artillery, the Allied force advanced on Krithia, located at the base of the flat-topped hill of Achi Baba, starting at noon on May 6th. The attack was launched from a beachhead on Cape Helles, where troops had landed on April 25th to begin the large-scale land invasion of the Gallipoli Peninsula after a naval attack on the Dardanelles failed miserably in mid-March. Since the first failed attempt on the village, Hunter-Weston's original force had been joined by two brigades of the Australian and New Zealand Army Corps (ANZAC) to bring the total number of men to 25,000. They were still outnumbered, however, by the

Turkish forces guarding the town, which were under the direct command of the German Major-General Erich Weber. Weber had been promoted from the rank of colonel after supervising the closure and mining of the Dardanelles six months earlier.

Facing superior enemy numbers and suffering from a shortage of ammunition, the Allies were able to advance some 600 yards but failed to capture either Krithia or the crest of Achi Baba after three attempts in three days. Hunter-Weston's troops suffered heavy losses, with a total of 6,000 casualties. The two British naval brigades engaged in the battle saw half their number, some 1,600 soldiers, killed or wounded.

The British regional commander in chief, Sir Ian Hamilton, after pushing for more supplies and ammunition, ordered Hunter-Weston to continue the pressure on Achi Baba and a third attack on the ridge was launched in early June. As heavy casualties continued to be sustained across the region, with few real gains for the Allies, it became clear that the Gallipoli operation—an Allied attempt to break the stalemate on the Western Front by achieving a decisive victory elsewhere—had failed to achieve its ambitious aims.

By the time Bruhn's troopship steamed into the Dardanelles, his battalion had been relieved at Helles and sent back to Anzac Cove, a place a soldier didn't particularly want to be. The terrain was a myriad of steep escarpments, deep ravines and narrow gullies descending to an exposed beach.

The trenches were crowded with open latrines, flies and the ubiquitous rats scampering about looking for food quite often feasting on human flesh.

Charles Bean observed in his book *The Story of Anzac*:

> *In these deep narrow alleys the front-line troops and supports lived as completely enclosed as in the lanes of a city, having their habitations along them in niches undercut in the wall, sometimes curtained by hanging blankets or waterproof sheets. Meanwhile the company and battalion headquarters, the medical aid-post, the quartermaster's store, and other offices became gradually as fixed and recognised as the public offices of a metropolis. The bivouacs on slopes behind the lines resembled the clustered booths at a great fair. In some respects most men came to regard the routine as one of city life.*

When Bruhn landed at Anzac Cove he was astonished. The Turks commanded all the high ground and in some areas, there were only three yards between the belligerents. The Turks also seemed to have superior weapons including heavy artillery.

His commanding officer, Major Archie Webster, identified Norman as a crack shot. He was assigned to be a sniper, aided by Darcy Smith, one of his mates he befriended on the ship. Darcy would use a telescope to identify the target and Norman would shoot him with his Lee Enfield with a telescopic sight. The duo became known as the most lethal sniper pair on the ridge.

Norman Bruhn lasted just a couple of months before he was hospitalised with influenza at Mudros, a small port on the Greek island of Lemnos. Illness was rife among the Anzac troops that July, with hundreds of men hospitalised with dysentery and fever.

Mudros Hospital

The crowded tent hospitals of Mudros were claustrophobic, especially once the dysentery cases began arriving. Norman stayed in for eleven days and he was discharged just in time to join his comrades in the Battle of Lone Pine in August. The 2nd Brigade distinguished itself in this engagement; winning nine Victoria Crosses. Norman wasn't one of the recipients. In September the 6th Battalion was relieved and sent to Lemnos. There, on the 17th, Norman Bruhn was readmitted to hospital, suffering flu. He re-joined his battalion on the 6th of November.

Back in Egypt after the Anzac forces evacuated Gallipoli in December, Bruhn went Absent Without Leave early in the New Year and as a result received 28 days of field punishment number 2. This meant that he was handcuffed, and possibly fettered as well, and forced to carry out heavy labour. Unpleasant as that undoubtedly was, it was still an improvement on field punishment number 1, in which the offender was not only shackled but also tied to a fixed object such as a gun wheel for up to two hours at a time. If the army manual was followed to the letter, the offender's arms would be outstretched and his legs bound together, giving the appearance of crucifixion.

In late February, Bruhn was assigned to the 46th Battalion, formed from Gallipoli veterans and reinforcements newly arrived from Australia. In late March, the new battalion marched out to Serapeum, in the desert near the Suez Canal. The Turks had been active in this area, and the 46th's job was to help defend it.

It was a ridiculous exercise to march in 100-degree heat with a full pack and inadequate water for three days. The sand was soft and deep, and the sun was scorching, with many of the men collapsed along the way.

Norman had had enough. He went AWOL for four days. Where he was, nobody knew but he earned himself seven days in gaol and forfeited five days' pay.

He was only out of confinement for two days before he disappeared again, this time for a month. He made the best of his freedom in Cairo getting drunk and getting laid. He returned to Mena Camp and received 28 days in confinement and forfeited 30 days' pay.

When released he was shipped to France, to join the rest of his battalion fighting the Germans up north.

In France he continually went AWOL. Each time he was eventually arrested, gaoled, fined and re-joined his battalion until the next offence, which usually wasn't long coming.

In early September 1916 Bruhn was admitted to hospital with myalgia (muscle pain), then on the 15th of September, discharged. Three days later he was off again, and not sighted until the 14th of November. He was found lying down drunk seven kilometres from a base in woods at Camiers. One of the arresting officers told the subsequent court martial that Bruhn 'smelt strongly of drink' and became 'very abusive' as he was being 'assisted' to a lorry for the drive back to detention at Étaples.

He was sentenced to two years imprisonment with hard labour. Only a couple of weeks later the sentence was suspended, probably because Bruhn's battalion was moving on. The 46th was briefly at Dernancourt, then St Vaast, where their time was filled with general training and musketry while they waited for their next engagement.

A week after re-joining his unit, just before New Year's Eve, Norman Bruhn broke camp and went missing until the second week of February. He was now classed as a deserter.

A dose of the clap landed Bruhn in hospital in Étaples in early March 1917. There he stayed for almost seven weeks before re-joining his unit, only to last a day before being readmitted under arrest to hospital for 'VDG' (venereal disease, gonorrhoea). This became the pattern of Bruhn's war, shuffling constantly between the field punishment compound, the hospital, then back to his unit, where he would break out again.

He had been AWOL for more than two months when the Armistice was declared on the 11th of November 1918. On the 23rd of November he was arrested, and a few days later admitted to hospital at Le Havre for VD. He escaped again and was eventually arrested at Amiens in February 1919. He was held there by the provost marshal, 'pending disposal', but then escaped from the escort taking him back to his unit.

At last, on the 23rd of October 1919, he was sent to England. Eight days later he was court-martialled in London, charged with being AWOL in France between the 29th of March and the 17th of October. He was sentenced to nine months detention and admitted to Lewes Detention Barracks. A bit over a month later, he was shipped home, and the unexpired portion of his sentence was remitted. The authorities had washed their hands of him.

Norman Bruhn's war finally ended on the 4th of February 1920 when the disgraced digger disembarked in Melbourne and was handed his discharge papers, stamped 'Services no longer required'. Befitting his misconduct, Bruhn forfeited his entitlement to the standard military decorations and medals. The only reminders of his war service were his scars and tattoos. On his left forearm, '1915' and 'Egypt' was inscribed above and below a Union Jack and a French flag.

Norman knew what career he would undertake when he arrived in Melbourne; it would be a life of crime.

He soon discovered that one man dominated the underworld in Melbourne in 1920. His name was Squizzy Taylor.

Norm had heard on the streets that Squizzy frequented a pub in Richmond, so he purchased a dark suit from Leviathan Men's Wear in Bourke Street and made his way to the *Richmond Arms Hotel* in Bridge Road. Norman entered the bar and ordered a beer.

He addressed the barman.

'I'm looking for Squizzy Taylor, mate. Can you tell me if he's here?'

'No, but I expect he'll arrive any minute now. He usually sits over there with his band of brothers.'

'What do you mean— a band of brothers? Does he come from a large family?'

'No, mate. It's just what they call each other. They're not really related.'

'Can I ask a favour? When he arrives can you let me know?'

'I don't think you'll have any trouble identifying Squizzy and his cronies, but I'll give you the heads up when they come in. Why don't you take a seat close to where he normally sits?'

'Thanks, you've been most helpful.'

Norman waited for three more beers and finally a short thin bloke surrounded by big burly muscle types entered the bar. Norman looked over at the barman who gave him a nod. Norm waited until they settled in, each with a beer in their hands. He approached the group.

Squizzy, Frank and Sam

'Excuse me, sir, I believe you are known as Squizzy Taylor?'

'I might be. Who the fuck are you?'

'My name is Norman Bruhn. I've just returned from the war. I'm looking to join a gang, and I hear yours is the best in Melbourne.'

'You heard right. What can you bring to the party?'

'I was enlisted in the army for four years, so I know how to fight. I was imprisoned several times for various crimes, which indicates my lack of respect for authority. I would be a loyal member of the gang and do everything you ask of me.'

'I'll tell you what— What's your fucking name again?'

'Norman.'

'Okay, Norman I'll let you run with us for a week, then I'll decide if you stay, or I piss you off.'

'Thanks, Squizzy.'

'This here's Frank. You can hang onto his coattails; do everything he asks of you.'

Frank, a large man with a round face, pulled Norman aside.

'We've got a job on this Saturday night. We're hitting a jewellery store in the city; you can act as a lookout. Are you fine with that?'

'No problem Frank.'

The robbery at Zamia's Jewellery store went off without a hitch and the gang netted £2000. Norman conducted his duties admirably and got the sign off from Frank.

Norman had one more test before being accepted into Squizzy's gang. He was to accompany Frank on a visit to a drug dealer who purchased cocaine from the gang. The dealer had not paid the gang for the last shipment, claiming it was inferior, having been cut with boric acid.

The two men arrived at Ben Hasseldorf's house in Collingwood, knocking loudly on the front door.

Ben eventually opened up.

'Good evening Ben, can we come in?' asked Frank.

'That depends on what you want.'

'I think it would better to discuss it inside, Ben.'

'I suppose so; come in.'

Ben led the two gangsters into his kitchen at the back of the house. The three men sat at the kitchen table.

'The reason we have paid you a visit is that you owe Squizzy £50, and we'd like to get it from you tonight.'

'That last shipment was useless. You bastards cut it with boric.'

'We believe that's what you do to every shipment you purchase from us before you take it to the streets.'

'Okay, I admit that, but I wasn't able to cut it any more. I had to flog it as is, cutting back my profit margin.'

'Look, I tell you what I can do, Ben. You pay me the £50 and we'll leave you alone but if you decide not to pay us we'll beat you so badly you won't be able to get out of bed for a fucking month. It's up to you. Either way, I can assure you we'll get our 50 quid.'

'Fuck it! All right, I'll get your fucking money. You stay here while I get it.'

'That's more like it, Ben.'

Ben left the kitchen and was absent for about five minutes. He returned with the £50. As Frank was counting the money on the kitchen table, Ben pulled out a revolver from his pocket and aimed it at Frank.

Norman reacted quickly, grabbing the gun and forcing it out of the dealer's hand. He then pistol-whipped Ben across the face, knocking him to the floor. Norman placed his foot on his head, holding him down.

'What should I do with this scum, Frank?'

'Kick him in the head a few times, son, but don't kill the bastard.'

Norman obliged.

Frank and Norman left the drug dealer in a pool of blood on the kitchen floor. They returned to Squizzy's Richmond house and recounted what had happened.

Squizzy Taylor's House

'Well, boys, you did well—especially you, Norman. Consider yourself one of the gang.'

Norman became a valuable member of Squizzy's gang, known for his expertise in bashing and shooting.

Norman was given the task of shooting Ted Healy, a rival gang member from the notorious Fitzroy Gang. The police arrested Norman and hauled him before the Magistrate's Court where he was given bail. He decided it would be a safer option to abscond to Sydney and lie low for a while. This decision proved to be a turning point in the gangster's life.

The case was dismissed due to a lack of evidence.

A CHANGE IS AS GOOD AS A HOLIDAY

Norman boarded the train at Spencer Street Station, bound for Central Station Sydney— a twelve-hour journey. He knew one person in Sydney; Ned Thompson, who had been in the same battalion as Norman and was in trouble with the brass almost as much as Norman. Norm had written to his mate informing him of his imminent arrival in the harbour city.

As the train pulled up to platform 1, Norm looked out the carriage window and saw Ned sitting on a bench seat.

The train pulled to a halt. Norm stepped off the carriage onto the platform and greeted his old army mate. Once he collected his suitcase, containing his life's possessions, they exited the magnificent station.

Ned rented a semi-detached house in Darlinghurst and that's where the two mates headed.

'Can I interest you in a nice cold beer mate?'

'Is the Pope a fucking Catholic?'

Ned cracked a bottle and poured two schooner glasses.

'So what's the score in Sydney town, Ned? Who rules the roost?'

'Well, believe it or not, two fucking sheilas are the kingpins or should I say queen pins. Tilly Devine runs about twenty brothels plus a cocaine operation. She has a bloody big gang which has no hesitation in using its muscle.

'Her arch-rival is Kate Leigh. She also operates brothels but her main line of business is sly-grog shops. Having said that she rivals Tilly's cocaine business. Kate also runs a mean gang.'

'So do you reckon we can move in and take some of the action?' asked Norman.

'We'd have to be bloody careful but yes, I think we could do it.'

'I reckon if we could entice a couple of the Melbourne boys to come up to Sydney we'd then be a force to be reckoned with.'

'Who do you think we could get?' asked Ned.

'Snowy Cutmore for a start, plus George Wallace and Jack Hayes.'

Snowy Cutmore

GEORGE WALLACE

70

'Well, That would be a bloody good start. Those boys are tough sons of bitches.'

'Yeah, they won't take shit from anybody.'

'When are you bringing the wife and kids over here, mate?'

'They're arriving next week. To tell you the truth I really miss them.'

Norman's wife, Irene, was a dressmaker and he adored their two boys, Noel and Keith. Norman separated his family life from his cutthroat existence as a gangster.

He rented a flat in Paddington close enough to the action but far enough away to keep his family from danger.

Once the rest of the gang arrived in Sydney it didn't take long for the razor gang to become established and feared in Kings Cross and Darlinghurst.

Bruhn's gang was the first to use the cutthroat razor as their preferred weapon.

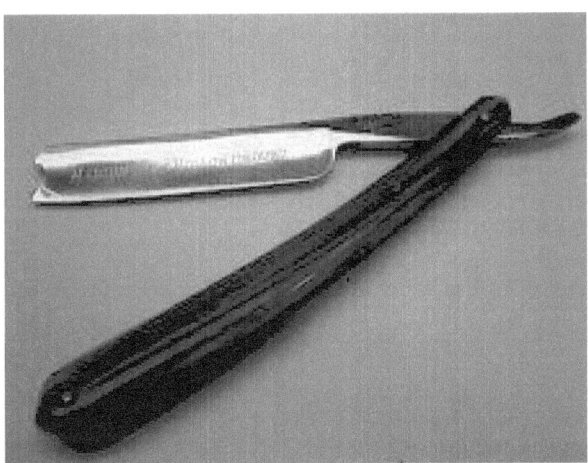

The Bruhn gang decided the first hit would be Tilly Devine's street girls. Despite operating several brothels in and around Darlinghurst, Jim Devine and his lovely wife pimped a large number of girls on the streets of Kings Cross and Darlinghurst.

The razor gang, as they became known, would approach a prostitute with their blades drawn. Holding a razor against the girl's cheek they would demand the night's takings.

This proved to be extremely effective, but it earned the wrath of Tilly and Jim Devine. The razor gang war was about to commence.

Between 1927 and 1930 there were more than 500 razor attacks recorded. How many went unrecorded was unknown.

'Snowy I want you to come with me and bring George and Jack.'

'Sure, Norm. What's going on?'

'That slut Leigh is proving to be a real thorn and we need to sort her out.'

'What do you plan to do?'

'Kate is too protected to get to her, but we can rough up some of her gang. That might teach her to pay us what is due.'

'So what's the plan, Norm?'

'Her gang drink at the *Tradesman's Arms Hotel* in Darlinghurst. I plan to attack them as they're leaving the pub with a skin full.'

'That sounds like a plan,' said Snowy.

'Make sure your razors are nice and sharp. We want to give them all a clean shave.'

The four standover men made their way to the hotel, which was located in Palmer Street, right smack in the middle of Kate Leigh's vice empire.

Norm instructed his men to wait on the corner of Liverpool Lane and Palmer Street where they had a clear view of the *Tradesman's Arms* without being conspicuous.

Right on 6 o'clock, the drinkers began pouring out of the hotel. Most would be moving on to one of Kate's sly-grog shops to continue drinking to all hours.

Norm recognised Red Harrison. He stood out in the crowd with his bright red hair, which he wore longer than the fashion of the time. With him were two other gang members, although Norm didn't know their names.

Norm signalled to his men to follow him. They approached the men from behind, trying to be as quiet as possible.

Norm yelled, 'Hey Red.'

Big Red turned around only to be slashed from ear to ear with Norm's razor. He fell to the footpath, holding his throat, with blood oozing between his fingers.

Snowy took Norm's lead, slashing of one of the other Leigh gang members across the face from ear to chin. Finally, George slashed the third and final member of the group.

Norm stood over the bleeding trio and instructed them to tell Kate to pay her monthly protection fee or there would be more of the same.

The razor gang left the scene before the cops were called.

Things were only to get worse in some respects and better in others.

NELL MY BELLE

CHAPTER 13

Napoleon suffered his greatest defeat at Waterloo in Belgium in June 1815.

In Sydney, Australia, in the inner suburb of Waterloo, a beautiful baby girl was born in 1910. Her parents named her Nellie.

Colin and Lillian Kelly divorced soon after Nellie began attending school. Lillian married Robert Cameron and Nellie adopted her stepfather's name for the remainder of her life.

Nellie lived a normal life. She was a bright student achieving good grades at Monte Sant'Angelo Mercy College, an exclusive north shore school.

She mixed well with the other children and caused no real trouble to her parents.

Then puberty arrived and with it, her behaviour completely changed in every way. She became disobedient to both her parents and her teachers. She refused to complete her homework and flirted with the male teachers.

FEBRUARY 1926

Lillian arrived home from the grocery shopping, expecting to find Nellie, but her daughter was nowhere to be seen. Lillian assumed Nellie was visiting one of her school friends, but when she didn't arrive home for dinner she and Robert became concerned.

Nellie had decided that fifteen was old enough to live her own life and she made her way to King Cross to begin her new career.

It did not occur to the police that she might be living in Sydney's major red-light district.

The first task the young girl completed was to buy suitable clothing, which would attract clients. Once suitably attired as a whore she waited on a street corner, hoping to attract her first customer.

Nellie didn't have to wait long; a middle-aged man in a blue suit approached the girl.

'Hello, darling, would you be interested in making me a happy man?'

'How would I do that?'

'Come back with me to my hotel and I'll show you, sweetheart.'

'It will cost you ten shillings.'

'Looking at how young and beautiful you are I would say it will be money well spent.'

'So which hotel are you staying at, darling?'

'*The Strand* in Darlinghurst.'

'Good-oh. That's just a few blocks away.'

That night Nellie gained her first immoral earnings as well as losing her virginity. The beautiful girl was on her way to a life of whoring and violence. She was only fifteen.

Nellie did not align herself with a pimp despite Tilly Devine and Kate Leigh pressuring her to join their stables.

Nellie Cameron

She soon became known as Sydney's most popular and expensive prostitute.

Nellie discovered she had an attraction to dangerous and violent men and her first boyfriend was Norman Bruhn. Norman was infatuated with the young and beautiful Nellie. He showered her with gifts including expensive jewellery. His wife Irene received no such gifts.

Bruhn got his return on investment in spades. He charged Nellie protection money, and a percentage of everything she earned went into Bruhn's pocket.

Nellie accommodated on average ten customers a day seven days a week. Her earnings before Bruhn took his cut were £35 a week when the average wage was £3 a week. A large part of her income went on flamboyant clothes.

It was obvious Bruhn did not follow suit as he was a very dour dresser.

The pair became known as the power couple around the pubs and clubs in Sydney's eastern suburbs including Kings Cross.

Norman Bruhn and his henchmen, George Wallace, Snowy Cutmore and Razor Jack Hayes, would drink in their local pub to the point of inebriation then bail up the local sly-grog shop or prostitutes or a local drug dealer and demand their night's earnings. If they were refused the gang would slash the faces of their quarry and on occasion kill them.

Bruhn would then visit Nellie, boasting about his criminal activities. They would have sex then Bruhn would go home to his wife and children.

'Hello, Nellie my girl, have you got a cold beer and a hot body for your man?'

'Of cause I do, Normie. What would you like first, babe?'

'Tempting as it is to choose the other I'll go for a beer first if you don't mind. It's been a busy night.'

Nellie took a bottle of beer from the ice chest, opened it and poured Norman a beer with plenty of froth on top.

'So babe, what did you get up to tonight? Make lots of money?'

'The boys and I hit a sly-grog shop and we fair cleaned the bastards out.'

'Did you hurt anybody, love?'

'No, they were as weak as piss. They handed over the dosh as soon as they caught sight of our blades.'

'Good one, darl. Hurry up and finish your beer. I'm in the mood to be fucked.'

'Come here, sweetheart. I've got something special for you and I don't mean perfume.'

The two lovers moved into the bedroom and thrashed about for a good hour.

Norman then went home to his wife and happy family in Paddington.

DECEMBER 1926

Cutmore, Wallace and a couple of Bruhn's gang members were looking for easy money in the Darlinghurst area when they came across a young whore waiting for her next job.

'Hello love, how's business tonight?' asked Cutmore.

'Not bad. The Christmas period is always pretty good. Why do you ask?'

'Well, we would like to relieve you of your takings as a Xmas present to us,' said Wallace.

'You can get fucked. I worked hard for that money. I'm not about to give it to the likes of you.'

'See this nice new razor? How would you like me to slice your pretty face open with it?'

A young boxer, Billy Chalmers, had arrived on the scene and hearing what was being said he pushed Wallace in the chest and hit Cutmore square on the nose causing a nosebleed. The rest of the gang took off.

They all met back at the *Tradesman's Arms* furious at what had happened.

'That prick needs a bloody good lesson. He had no right to interfere with our business,' said Cutmore.

'I agree. We need to teach him what's what,' said Wallace.

'Not only that we have our reputation to protect. You can bet your balls word has already got out.'

'I think Christmas morning would be an appropriate time to pay Chalmers a visit and deliver him his present,' said Wallace.

DECEMBER 25

Bruhn, together with Wallace and Cutmore, broke into Chalmers's Darlinghurst flat early on Christmas morning with revenge on their minds.

'Chalmers wake up, you bastard. Santa has a present for you.'

'What in the fuck are you bastards doing here? Get out.'

Billy attempted to throw them out, but Cutmore pistol-whipped him on the back of his head, rendering the boxer unconscious.

Bruhn took his razor and sliced Chalmers's leg from top to bottom, ensuring all the tendons were severed. The gang then robbed the young boxer of anything that was of any real worth.

Billy Chalmers spent the Christmas of 1926 in hospital having 76 stitches in his leg.

He could never box again. It was the end of a promising career.

THE BATTLE OF THE RAZORS

Phil (the Jew) Jeffs was one of the four gangsters who controlled the crime scene in Sydney.

Jeffs was a smart operator who dominated the Sydney cocaine scene. He also ran several brothels in competition to Tilly Devine and Kate Leigh.

He stayed away from Tilly and Kate, respecting their operations, but he detested Norman Bruhn.

He ran his own razor gang that had no hesitation in slashing an adversary.

The Sydney gangs had survived due to a truce among thieves and whores. Tilly, Kate, Norman, and Phil the Jew had an unwritten agreement not to demarcate onto the others' territories.

The agreement was broken by Norman Bruhn in March 1927. He intended to increase his slice of the gangland pie.

A black Oldsmobile was cruising slowly down Palmer Street looking for prey, driven by one of Kate Leigh's henchmen. Three men from Bruhn's gang, including George Wallace, jumped onto the running board.

'Pull over, you fat prick. I want your dosh. Hand it over or I'll slash your fucking throat,' Wallace demanded.

'Okay, you can have all that I've got.'

'How much is that?'

'Five shillings each; that's it.'

'Five shillings, get fucked! Cutmore, pin the bastard down while I give him a shave.'

Wallace slashed the poor driver from his forehead down his left cheek to his chin and down to his mouth. To add insult to injury Wallace stole the poor bastard's wallet.

The victim's name was Tom White. He received 45 stitches.

After several weeks Tom's injuries had healed, although he would be scarred for life.

One Friday he entered *Brown's Tobacconists* to purchase a tin of pipe tobacco. To his delight he saw George Wallace in the shop. Since the attack, he always carried a Colt Revolver provided to him by Kate Leigh.

'Remember me, you fat ugly bastard?'

Tom pressed the barrel into Wallace's stomach, threatening to shoot the gangster.

Wallace ran from the shop calling for the police to save him and squealing like a girl.

A few weeks later, White was drinking in a Darlinghurst hotel when Wallace entered the bar. White pulled out his revolver and fired at point-blank range, but unfortunately, the pistol jammed. Wallace laughed and pulled out his trusty razor, slashing White on his right cheek. He now had matching cheeks.

FEBRUARY 1927

Norman Bruhn and his gang of thugs were enjoying a meal in the dining room of the *Tradesmen's Arms*. The purpose of the meeting was to plan their next step in becoming the unchallenged number one criminal gang in Sydney.

'I reckon one of the first things we need to take care of is Sid Kelly. The bastard has become a bit too big for his boots,' said Bruhn.

'I don't think Phil Jeffs is going to like us roughing up his best mate, Norman,' said Cutmore.

'I don't give a flying fuck what Jeffs thinks he's gunna be next.'

'Fair enough, mate.'

'Right now, I want Hayes to track Kelly down and cut his fucking throat. You right with that Hayes?'

'No love lost between me and Kelly or his mad brother for that matter, Norm,' agreed Hayes.

Razor Jack Hayes took off in pursuit of his quarry. He knew Kelly frequented the Victoria Royal Hotel. He waited outside in a laneway opposite the hotel from where he had an excellent view of the entrance to the public bar. Just on 6 pm Kelly exited the pub walking down Hargraves Street. His intention was to call into one of Phil Jeffs' sly-grog shops and continue drinking.

Hayes followed the gangster for a block, then grabbed him from behind, running his razor across the unsuspecting Kelly's throat. Kelly dropped to the footpath, with blood streaming from his wound.

The prick won't last long. I better get out of here before the cops arrive, he thought.

It didn't take long for the police to arrive. They placed the injured thug into a police wagon, racing him to St Vincent's Hospital. Ironically Kelly survived to fight another day.

Sid and his brother, Tom, began to plan their revenge almost immediately after Sid was discharged from the hospital. Both brothers were street brawlers, so they knew how to fight.

The brothers knew that Bruhn and his gang frequented a sly-grog shop owned by Joe McNamara. The place was also known for its cocaine and other drugs.

Sid and Tom waited outside the establishment until they spotted Bruhn and the bastard that slashed Sid's throat, Razor Jack Hayes, to enter. The brothers followed them in. The Kellys picked a fight with Bruhn and Hayes, beating the shit out of their adversaries. Both men were hospitalised.

Once Bruhn was discharged from hospital he began planning his new operation. As far as he was concerned, Tilly Devine, Kate Leigh, and Phil Jeffs were fair game. Let the war begin.

GANG WARFARE

CHAPTER 15

MARCH 1927

'Nellie, I think I know what I need to do to ensure I become the king of the Sydney scene. We need to hit our opposition hard and fast and scare the bastards out of the market. What do you think, babe?'

'I've got my mouth full, honey. You finish up and I'll give you my opinion.'

'Oh sorry, babe, here you go.'

'I think you're right, but scaring Tilly, Kate and Jeffs won't be an easy task,' said Nellie, wiping her mouth with a silk handkerchief.

'Yeah, I know but my gang has the balls to do it. They won't know what hit them. I'll call the boys together and start planning the raids in the next few days.'

'Anything I can do to help, babe?'

'I might get you to lure a few of their gang members into a compromising position if you know what I mean.'

'Yes, I think I know what you mean.'

Bruhn sent out messages to his key gang members, Snowy Cutmore, George Wallace and Razor Jack Hayes. The gang comprised another six thugs they could call on when needed.

They met in the back room of the *Tradesmen's Arms* in Darlinghurst.

Norman sat at the head of the table. Each member of the gang had a glass of whisky in front of him.

'The reason I called you all together is to formulate a plan which will ensure we become the top gang in Sydney from now fucking on. Has anybody got any suggestions?'

'Yeah boss. We simply kill the gang leaders— you know, Tilly, Kate and Jeffs.'

'Well Snowy, that sounds simple enough, but they are all well protected so knocking them off may not be that easy.'

'Yeah, plus the fucking coppers would cotton on pretty quickly as to who's rubbing all these bastards out. They'd be knocking on our doors quick smart,' said George.

'I'll tell you what's going to happen, lads. We're going to raid every sly-grog shop and every brothel and intimidate their patrons to the point where they won't ever come back. We'll bleed Tilly, Kate and Jeffs dry. They'll be out of business by the end of the year.'

'When you say intimidate, boss, are we taking slashing and raping?' asked Razor Jack.

'Not so much the raping, Jack, but the odd slash with a razor will be acceptable.'

'That's a shame. I don't mind a good rape.'

APRIL 1927

Norman and Snowy drove to a Darlinghurst address, 15 Palmer Street, the location of one of Kate Leigh's sly-grog establishments. They obtained entry in the usual way via a password, and once inside they held razors against two of the patrons' necks.

'Listen up you bastards, we want you to leave this joint right now. We can assure you we'll be back, and we may not be so nice next time. Fuck off.'

Kate's clients exited the sly-grog shop in haste. There was no doubt they wouldn't be returning anytime soon.

'That scared the shit out of them. Now let's rough the place up a bit and piss off before the cops arrive.'

Norman and Snowy broke all the spirit bottles and smashed the furniture. Once satisfied with their handiwork, they exited the building. One of Norman's gang was waiting outside in a Buick ready to spirit them away.

'Right, onto the next hit. Kate's going to be pissed.'

'Which one are we going to hit, boss?'

'Twenty-One Crown Street; the jewel in her crown.'

Norm had arranged for three more of the gang to meet them outside. Included was George Wallace, the hardest, meanest member of the gang.

A lesser-known gangster, Frank Wilson, approached the door and uttered the password, "Mum's in". The door opened and Bruhn's gang stormed in.

'Everybody down on the floor. If anyone of you lifts your head we'll blow the fucking head off. Is that clear?' yelled Norman.

Norman forced the barman to open the till and once it was cleared he and his gang forced Kate's customers to leave the joint. They then trashed the place and left.

Kate Leigh was sitting in her living room sharing a whisky with her long-time lover Wally Tomlinson when there was a loud knock on the front door. Wally got up to answer it, a razor in his hand in case it was unwelcome company.

'Who is it?'

'Wally, it's Jim Jones. Let me in. I need to talk to Kate.'

Wally unlocked the door, letting his comrade in.

'Kate, two of your grog shops have been hit.'

'What do you mean—hit?'

'Bruhn and his gang broke into Palmer and Crown Streets, wrecking both places and robbing the tills.'

'What the fuck does he think he's doing? I'll kill the prick.'

While Kate Leigh was planning Norman Bruhn's demise he was planning a hit on Tilly Devine's brothels. The first house of ill repute was in Crown Street; a three-storey terrace. Norman knocked on the front door, and a beautiful young woman opened it, welcoming in what she thought was a party of four.

'Hello, darling, if you want to remain beautiful you'll tell us how many patrons are on the job as it were. If you don't cooperate I'll get one of my boys to slash your pretty face.'

'There are ten rooms and they're all occupied at the moment.'

'Where's the madam?'

'That's me tonight. Lucy had to go home as one of her kids was sick.'

'All right boys, knock on every door and get the punters down here in the parlour. If they don't open the door knock the fucker down.'

Eventually, all the clients had dressed and assembled in the parlour.

'Listen up, you bastards. My name is Norman Bruhn. I'm the meanest toughest son of a bitch you will ever meet. Nobody will get hurt as long as you all cooperate. I want you to hand over your wallets to my men; I also want your watches.'

Fortunately, all the men cooperated, and they were permitted to leave the premises unhurt.

'Right, lovey, all we need now is the night's takings and then we'll be on our way.'

'I'm sorry. I don't have access to the safe. Only Tilly has the combination.'

'Is that right? Maybe a tickle with my razor might prod your memory.'

'I can't. I don't know it.'

'Is there any money kept outside the safe?'

'Just the takings from the last lot who visited.'

'Hand it over.'

The gang left with £200 and ten watches.

The gang moved on to another Tilly Devine establishment in Hill Street, Darlinghurst. Norman followed the same procedure, procuring twelve wallets and watches and the night's takings and this time he was able to unlock the safe.

The gang departed with booty of £500.

They planned to hit Jeffs' sly-grog shops the following night.

In the meantime, Tilly Devine and Kate Leigh arranged to meet to formulate a plan to eliminate Bruhn. They may have hated each other but they knew they needed to work together to get rid of this prick.

The meeting was arranged on neutral territory in a French restaurant in the city.

Tilly arrived at the restaurant first and asked the owner for a table at the back of the establishment.

Kate arrived a short time later and was shown to Tilly's table.

'Hello, Tilly, you're looking fit and well.'

'Cut the bullshit, Kate, and sit down.'

'I'm just trying to be civil.'

'Can I order you a drink?'

'Thanks. I'll have a double scotch on the rocks.'

'I might join you. I think we both need a stiff drink.'

Once the waiter brought them their drinks they began their discussion relating to Bruhn.

'Kate, I believe the bastard hit two of your establishments last night. He also trashed and robbed two of mine.'

'He did and I don't think he's going to stop there. We need to get rid of him.'

'I don't advise we use our gangs to complete the hit. My suggestion is we hire a professional hit man. That way it won't be linked to us.'

'Yes, I agree I have spent enough time in Long Bay.'

'Me too.'

'Do you have any suggestions as to who we hire?'

'Leave it with me, Kate. I'll get back to you.'

The two gangland matriarchs ordered their meals and were quite civil to each other through the evening.

Bruhn turned to the much-hated Jeffs for his next foray into enemy territory. He and three gang members including Snowy Cutmore and Jack Hayes held up a sly-grog shop in Liverpool owned in part by Jeffs. Phil the Jew as Jeffs was known was furious and he decided to hit back at the audacious Bruhns immediately.

Razor Jack Hayes exited the Darlinghurst pub just before 6pm. His intention was to continue drinking at a sly-grog shop around the corner.

As he walked along Liverpool Street, a black Oldsmobile pulled up beside him and called him over.

'G'day Jack, enjoying the early night air mate?'

''What's it fucking got to do with you?'

'Nothing. I just thought you might like this.'

One of the men in the car produced a revolver and shot Jack. He hit the footpath and lay in a puddle of blood. The car sped off, never to be seen again on Sydney streets.

A cab driver who witnessed the event lifted Hayes into his cab and drove him to hospital.

Jack survived the attack. Tom Kelly was arrested based on the cabbie's eyewitness account.

Kelly went to trial on the 28th of July 1928.

Jack had recovered well enough to partake.

Kelly's excuse was that Razor Jack had threatened to slash his face with a razor, so it was only self-defence.

Mr Edelman, the cab driver, testified, recounting what he had witnessed.

When Hayes was called to the stand, it was an entirely different story.

He declared both Edelman and Kelly were confused. He admitted to knowing Kelly but had never quarrelled with him. He told the court it certainly wasn't Kelly who shot him. In fact he had no idea who had pulled the trigger. He was summoned to a car and felt a sharp pain in his chest. The next thing he knew was when he woke up in hospital.

He admitted to knowing Bruhn but did not admit to being a member of his gang or slashing anyone.

The jury was totally confused once they had heard the three testimonies. They found the defendants not guilty.

THE WAR CONTINUES

CHAPTER 16

Bruhn was not intimidated by Hayes's shooting. His reaction was to escalate the war.

He didn't even wait for Hayes to be discharged from hospital. While his henchman was recovering, Bruhn and his gang hit one of Kate Leigh's sly-grog shops in Liverpool Street. The glint of the razors terrified Kate's patrons. They handed over their wallets and jewellery and they also robbed the manager of £100.

The next job, two days later, was also in Liverpool Street. The plan was to lay in wait for a notorious thief to arrive home. Bruhn knew he had pulled off a big robbery but hadn't organised Kate to fence it yet.

Bruhn and his gang demanded he hand over the cache and he did so without argument.

When Kate learned of the robberies she was even more infuriated. She knew she needed to act quickly.

Bruhn continued his violent rampage. He robbed another of Jeffs' sly-grog shops, taking a significant amount of cash plus cocaine.

Next on his list was Tilly Devine's brothels, harassing the girls and the patrons and in some instances assaulting both.

22 JUNE 1927

Norman Bruhn sat at the bar at the Courthouse Hotel drinking with Rob Miller, a horse trainer, Jim Hassett and Dick O'Brien. They had been drinking all day and as usual, Bruhn began arguing with the other three. Six o'clock closing time arrived and they staggered out of the hotel into Oxford Street.

Norman decided it was high time to visit Nellie Cameron again. He'd been a bit busy terrifying the city.

He arrived at Nellie's flat and knocked on her door.

'Who is it?'

'It's Norman, Nell, come on; let me in.'

'Hold on.'

Nellie opened the door in a sheer nightie.

'Geez, I've missed that, Nellie. You look great, babe.'

'Where the fuck have you been, Norman? It's over a month since I saw you last.'

'Don't be mad at me. I've been fucking busy. I bought you a present.'

'What is it?'

Let me in and I'll show you.'

'Okay, come in but you'd better behave. You're drunk.'

'I'm not drunk, Nellie— just slightly under the weather.'

Bruhn reached into his right pocket and extracted a beautiful gold and emerald bracelet.

'For you, my love.'

Norman, it's beautiful! It must have cost a fortune.'

'Nothing is too expensive for my Nellie.'

The fact was Bruhn had stolen the bracelet from the thief he had robbed who in turn had stolen it from a jewellery store. He had intended to give it to his wife but decided his best return on investment was with Nellie.

'Come here. I want to thank you properly.'

The two lovers had sex for an hour before Norman decided he should go home to his family.

Irene Bruhn was lying in bed waiting for her husband to come home. She heard three loud bangs from what she thought was close by. Irene put on a robe and went outside to investigate. A neighbour was already standing on the footpath.

'Hello, Sam did you hear those loud bangs? They sounded like gunshots to me.'

'Hello, Irene; no, I think it might have been a car backfiring. It's nothing to worry about so go back to bed.'

Irene went back to bed but couldn't get to sleep. At about midnight there was a knock on the door, and she rose to answer it.

Two policemen stood in front of her looking very grim.

'Mrs Bruhn, I'm afraid we have bad news. Your husband has been shot.'

'Oh my God, was he badly wounded?'

'He was killed, Mrs Bruhn. We're sorry to bring you such sad tidings.'

'I don't know what to say. I don't know what to do.'

Goodnight, Mrs Bruhn. Our deepest sympathies.

Nobody knew who had murdered Bruhn. The underworld as usual remained silent. Kate, Tilly and Jeffs the Jew were happy to see the bastard gone.

Bruhn didn't die immediately. A taxi raced him to hospital and as his life ebbed away a senior detective interviewed him, hoping to discover who fired the shots. Bruhn sent him away, stating he was no snitch. He died soon after.

His funeral was a small affair, as he wasn't much loved. Only Irene and his two brothers from Melbourne attended. He was buried at Rookwood cemetery in Sydney's west.

Irene was interviewed by a number of Sydney newspapers, and she was intent on clearing her deceased husband's name. There had been articles written about Bruhn which were defamatory.

'Mrs Bruhn, you must have been aware of your husband's activities as a notorious gangster.'

'Absolutely not! These horrible newspaper reports are wicked lies. If they were true, I would have been aware of it. Norman and I were married for seven wonderful years. He was a good husband and a good father to his children. There is no doubt he had his faults. After all, everybody does but I'm sure he never carried a razor or a gun. This is a man that enlisted to fight for his King and country. He fought and was severely wounded.'

'Mrs Bruhn, do you have any idea who killed your husband?'

'Yes, I do.'

'Have you informed the police?'

'No.

'Don't you want to exact revenge on your husband's killer?'

'No.'

'Why on earth not?'

'I want to stay alive for my children.'

At the coroner's inquest, after hearing several witnesses including Bruhn's drinking mates on the night of the shooting, and an intensive police hunt, a verdict of killing by an unknown assailant was declared.

Was it a coincidence that notorious Melbourne hitman, Harry Slater, had arrived in Sydney shortly before Bruhn's slaying?'

THE THREE AMIGOS

CHAPTER 17

1927

Kate Leigh, Tilly Devine and Phil Jeffs now had the city of Sydney at their criminal disposal and made good use of the opportunity. All three were making more money from sly-grog shops, brothels and cocaine than they had ever done before.

Not so fortunate was Razor Jack Hayes. After Bruhn died he couldn't keep out of trouble, and he was constantly involved in fights. After one particularly nasty fracas he immigrated to Germany and was never heard of again.

George Wallace was known around the traps as "The Midnight Raper", and after Bruhn's death he became a laughing stock around Darlinghurst.

His first encounter was with Tom Kelly.

'Hey, Kelly you fucking bastard, you killed my mate Norman Bruhn. I know it was you even though the fucking cops won't touch you. Well, I'll bloody touch you, fucking skinny prick.'

'You don't know what you're talking about, Wallace. It wasn't me. Mind you I'm happy to see the end of him I must admit.'

A fight broke out between the two adversaries. Wallace was the better boxer buy Kelly compensated by hurling a claw headed hammer at Wallace, hitting him directly on the forehead. Once Wallace got up from the footpath he hightailed it, leaving Kelly laughing at the sight of the overweight Wallace running down the street.

George Wallace

Wallace couldn't keep out of trouble his moments of sobriety were very limited plus his addiction to cocaine made matters worse.

One of the most popular nightclubs in Sydney was the *Plaza Café* in King Street. There was a cover charge of five shillings, but Wallace barged in refusing to pay.

The club's manager, Harry Murray, approached Wallace demanding he pay or leave the premises.

'Who's going to make me, you little upstart? Certainly not you.'

Wallace punched Murray in the face.

Wallace underestimated the manager's fighting ability and the two adversaries grappled on the floor as the club's patrons looked on in horror.

Murray's agility was giving him the upper hand. Wallace reached into his pocket and extracted his razor, slashing Murray's face.

'You fucking bastard, you've cut me. Someone call the cops.'

'Don't waste your time. The cops will take forever. I told you I'd do some damage— well how about this.'

Wallace proceeded to turn over tables and smash glasses against the wall.

'Stop it, don't be bloody stupid!' yelled Mary, a waitress at the club.

'Mind your own business, you bitch.'

Wallace picked up a heavy coffee pot, throwing it at Mary and striking her in the head. She began to bleed heavily.

Staff employed by the club locked the doors and called the police.

Knowing he was beaten Wallace slumped into a chair at the rear of the club. He began to cry and that's how the police found him.

'It wasn't my fault, officer. I'm completely innocent. The customers and staff attacked me for no good reason.'

'That's bullshit, officer. He started the fracas,' responded one of the crowd.

'Come on, Wallace, you can give a statement at the Darlinghurst Police Station; a place you are very familiar with.'

Wallace was brought before the court soon after. After pleading his innocence together with his responsibility for caring for his wife and five-month-old child he hoped to go free.

'George Wallace, you have been found guilty. You are fined £2.00 plus a further £3.00 for damages caused.'

George made a pledge to the court that he would reform his criminal ways and lead a good honest life.

He left Sydney soon after and left a trail of crime in Brisbane, Melbourne and Perth.

It was in Perth that he met his demise when he was stabbed by a miner who had been robbed of a significant amount by Wallace.

Now there was only one left from the infamous Bruhn gang. His name was Lancelot McGregor or otherwise known as Sailor the Slasher. He wasn't high in the pecking order of the gang but nevertheless he was brutal.

He decided to continue on in the protection game, terrorising all and sundry that crossed his path.

On September 13th, 1930, he entered *Ernie Good's Wine Bar* with the express purpose of demanding protection money from the owner.

'Give me five shillings or I'll slash your fucking face.'

'Piss off Saidler, I have no intention of paying you sixpence let alone five shillings.'

Saidler then threw a glass of red wine over Good's face.

'See this lovely razor? I'm going to slash your face with it, you arsehole.'

Good, not one to be intimidated easily, opened a drawer behind the bar and shot the antagonist in the forehead.

Saidler slumped to the ground he died five minutes later.

Good was arrested and tried but he was found not guilty on the grounds of self-defence.

The residents of Sydney's eastern suburbs were hopeful that the violence and crime would cease once Bruhn and his notorious gang were off the streets. Their hopes were dashed because the number of slashings and shootings actually increased, carried out not by the professional criminals of the underworld but by amateurs and petty criminals.

There were more than twenty shootings in the eastern suburbs in 1928 and many more razor attacks.

Tilly Devine, Kate Leigh and Phil Jeffs were looking to expand their criminal empires in the post Norman Bruhn world.

Phil Jeffs spent 1928 establishing a chain of sly-grog and cocaine shops in Kings Cross, Woolloomooloo and Darlinghurst. He continued his extortion business, demanding money from drug dealers, SP bookmakers and the girls on the streets. Phil the Jew was making a fortune.

He decided to establish several brothels in Darlinghurst in competition with Tilly Devine and Kate Leigh. The money kept rolling in.

Jeffs also enjoyed other pleasures, as did the members of his gang.

MARCH 5TH, 1928

Ida Mattocks, 28 and a mother of two, staggered into Darlinghurst Police Station obviously distraught and with her clothes torn.

'Please help me. I've been pack raped.'

'Okay, lady, take a seat and tell me what happened,' said the duty officer.

'I was walking down Bayswater Road on my way home when two men emerged from a lane.'

'Did they speak to you?'

'Yes, one said "hello love".'

'Did you respond?'

'No, I ignored him.'

'What about the other man?'

'He said, "Come here, dear".'

'So did you?'

'No, I quickened my pace hoping to get away from them, but they caught up with me, and then a third man appeared from nowhere.'

'So what happened next?'

'They grabbed me, shoving me down a lane way and into a block of flats.'

'I'm sorry, madam, but you need to tell me what happened in the flat.'

'Yes, I understand; the three of them raped me. I begged them to release me so I could go home to my husband and children. They just laughed at me and told me I could go home when they were through with me.'

'So they finally released you?'

'No, another man came into the bedroom and had his way with me.'

'Did they use their names while you were there?'

'The fourth one was called Phil.'

'That gives me a lead. I suggest you give me your name and address and go home. I'll keep you informed of our progress.'

The following day the police arrested Phil Jeffs, Ernest Wilson, Fred Payne, Les Heath and Herbert Wilson on a charge of rape and assault. If found guilty, they would all hang.

The *Sydney Morning Herald* reported the incident on its front page naming it "The Darlinghurst Outrage". The paper continued its coverage throughout the trial.

The five defendants could afford the best defence lawyers in Sydney. They argued that all the defendants had watertight alibis and therefore could not have been involved.

They also used character assassination against Ida Mattocks, stating she was a prostitute and was paid for her services.

The jury found all five defendants not guilty.

The police were furious, declaring they would get Jeffs somehow, somewhere.

Jeffs was arrested several times but continued to beat the charges.

KISS ME AGAIN KATE

CHAPTER 18

Kate Leigh in her prime was popular with the boys and she in turn enjoyed their company. She was a pretty young thing, slim waisted with large breasts.

By the time 1929 rolled around Kate had a weathered face and was fat with several chins. However her looks didn't detract from her success as one of Sydney's top gangsters.

Kate made it very clear to her employees who was boss. If one disobeyed her orders Kate was known to hit them over the head with whatever was handy; a brick, a tomahawk or a razor.

Kate's gravelly harsh voice could be heard bellowing in any one of her establishments.

Despite her terrorising manner, patrons flocked to Kate's sly-grog shops. Unlike the competition who watered down the grog Kate sold only the finest liquor. Sydneysiders didn't mind paying the exorbitant prices knowing they were drinking only the best.

Everybody needs a hobby. Kate's was to attend court hearings and while she peeled potatoes she yelled abuse at the accused and the lawyers defending them. This was a scene straight from *A Tale of Two Cities*.

Kate in Her 50s

Kate had established a formable gang of criminals to help her run her criminal empire.

The payroll included:

Gregory 'the gunman' Gaffney

Bernard 'Barney' Dalton

Wally Tomlinson (Leigh's lover)

May Seckold

Ivy Ryan

Vera Lewis

All had been involved in prostitution, drug pushing and sly-grog. Robbery and assault and battery were also part of their repertoire.

Bill Flanagan was Kate's knuckle man, responsible for kicking out unruly customers.

Finally but certainly not last, her chauffeur was a handsome young lad called Bruce Higgs. Rumour had it he was Kate's young bit on the side.

Bruce drove Kate to wherever she wanted to go in a black Studebaker. It looked more like a tank than a limousine.

Bruce was driving Kate to visit one of her establishments in Woolloomooloo when he brought up a very sensitive subject.

'Miss Leigh, I may not be able to drive you anymore.'

'Why not, Bruce? I thought you liked the job.'

'Oh, don't get me wrong I really enjoy driving you. I enjoy your company.'

'Then why do you want to stop?'

'I've been charged with murder along with my two brothers. If we are proved guilty I'll be in Long Bay for a bloody long while.'

'That's if they don't hang you first, Bruce. Did you do it?'

'No ma'am, I did not.'

'I'll help you with a bloody good lawyer. He'll help you beat it.'

'Thank you, ma'am.'

'You can stop calling me ma'am. My fucking name is Kate as well you know.'

'Sorry, Kate.'

'When you go to trial I'll give you a character reference.'

'Thanks, Kate.'

'Mr Evatt, my lawyer, will be in touch with you shortly and in the meantime you can keep driving for me.'

The charge against Bruce and his brothers entailed the murder of a retired grazier, Ronald Leslie in the Blue Mountains. The police downgraded the murder charge against Bruce and his brother Hubert to "accessories to murder". Their elder brother William was charged with murder.

There were no witnesses to the shooting and no real supporting evidence and as a consequence all were found not guilty.

Bruce didn't see the error of his ways, continuing to be a loyal employee of the infamous Kate Leigh and as a consequence he was arrested several times, spending stints in Long Bay Gaol.

Long Bay Gaol

BATTLE OF BLOOD ALLEY

CHAPTER 19

Blood Alley, Kings Cross

Phil Jeffs was a greedy man and despite making significant profits from selling cocaine he wanted more. He decided to cut the cocaine with boracic acid, selling it as pure and therefore increasing his return on investment.

Boracic acid is a lethal poison used for insect repellent. Drug pushers use it to cut cocaine because the crystals look very similar to the drug they call "snow". Many of Jeffs' clients fell sick while others died.

A rival gang who purchased Phil Jeffs' cocaine to on-sell to their own customers discovered his deception and threw down the gauntlet, challenging Jeffs and his gang to a fight.

Phil accepted the challenge. Blood Alley was chosen as the venue; named for its reputation as a street-fighting venue.

It was late in the evening when the rival gangs met in Blood Alley. It was a frightening sight.

Jeffs' gang had taken the high ground on the southern end armed with pistols, baseball bats and razors.

The Eastern Push as they called themselves was similarly armed and positioned on the northern end of the alley. They were relegated to the lower ground.

'Jeffs, are you and your motley crew ready to get the shit beat out of you? We'll teach you a lesson not to dud us.'

'You bastards won't know what hit you. You're dealing with Phil Jeffs now, you bunch of pricks.

'Right fellas, let's get them,' shouted Jeffs.

Phil Jeffs led from the front and his crew of twenty gangsters followed. Jeffs carried a Colt 45 pistol in his right hand and his favourite razor, The Gauntlet, in his left.

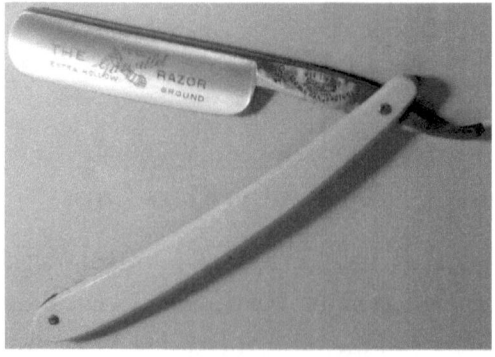

His gang carried an eclectic arsenal including razors, machetes, and baseball bats. William Archer, Jeffs' second in command, carried a shotgun. The gang was ready to take out The Eastern Push.

The Push, also armed to the hilt with similar weapons, approached their adversaries with revenge in mind.

As the two groups met a wild brawl began. No participant escaped unscathed as Blood Alley lived up to its name and reputation.

William Archer became the first major casualty when he received a gunshot wound to the right leg. His would-be assassin was Charles Sorley. When Archer bleeding profusely attempted to escape the melee by jumping onto the running board of a passing car, Sorley dragged him off and began laying in his boot until Archer lost consciousness.

Jeffs saw what had happened to his mate, and he and three of his men laid into Sorley with savage abandon. After thirty minutes of brawling, the police arrived in numbers breaking up the donnybrook.

Archer was transported to St Vincent's Hospital via ambulance. When he had recovered to the point where police could interview him he told them he had no idea who had shot him.

Jeffs and a number of other men were arrested and taken to Darlinghurst Police Station. Jeffs was charged with assaulting Frederick Johns and was bailed on £100. Jeffs went home to his luxurious Kensington home and retired to bed. It had been a long night.

The next morning he woke in St Vincent's Hospital with two bullet wounds in his shoulder and chest. Neighbours had heard gunshots early in the morning and had investigated. They found Jeffs writhing about on his front lawn and one neighbour called for an ambulance and the police.

The police were able to question Jeffs once he had been stabilised by hospital staff.

'Well Phil, it seems you have a few enemies, mate,' said Sergeant Bailey.

'Tell me something new, officer.'

'Have you got any idea who shot you?'

'Normally I wouldn't say, but I don't think I'm long for this world so what the fuck. It was Jim Taylor and Bill Clark.'

'Why did they shoot you, Phil?'

'Money, it's always fucking money. They demanded I hand over my cash. I told them I didn't have any and they got angry and shot me.

'They pissed off out my bedroom window. I chased after them but only got as far as the front lawn.'

The police tracked down the two assailants, arresting them for attempted murder. Phil recovered and was seen as the prime witness in their trial.

When questioned by the prosecutor Phil denied his initial statement, saying it was a complete fabrication. The assailant could not be identified, as it was too dark.

Taylor and Clark were found not guilty.

Queen of the Whores

Tilly Devine, the girl from the slums of London who stole cream buns from her classmates, had developed into Sydney's most successful madam with thirty brothels under her management.

She hadn't achieved this success by being sweet and innocent. She was a hard-nosed businesswoman who would steal from her patrons' wallets without any guilt and arrange for one of her goons to beat up any troublesome customers.

Ever mindful of the possibility of robbery or drunken unruly customers, Tilly installed steel grates on all the ground floor windows of her brothels.

Each brothel had a manager or madam to oversee the business. She was responsible for ensuring the girls were safe and customers were well behaved. Tilly provided each madam with a loaded pistol just in case.

Tilly enjoyed her "Queen of the Whores" status. She dressed in expensive yet gaudy clothes and each finger on her hands was embellished with several rings, usually diamonds. Tilly had her hair permed regularly to represent a porcelain doll; all curls. No matter how much money she had accumulated she was still a brash girl from the slums of London. Her language was atrocious as were her manners.

Tilly could be seen at Randwick racetrack chain-smoking and swigging whisky from a bottle; not very elegant.

Jim Devine continued his violent ways against his wife, constantly beating Tilly who despite the cuts and bruises would never testify against her husband.

In January 1931 Jim was charged with the attempted murder of his wife after the pair were engaged in a heated argument in their Maroubra home. Tilly escaped out onto the front lawn and Jim fired several shots at her as she ran onto the road. Jim was never regarded as a good shot even in the army and Tilly escaped unhurt. Her neighbours rang the police who arrived, quickly arresting Jim. He was released and acquitted of the charge as Tilly refused to testify.

Ten years later, the marriage split up. Tilly began a relationship with one of her criminal associates known as "Skinny Kenny" who became not only her lover but also her standover man.

In 1945, Tilly married Eric Parsons. She shot him in the leg just a few months before the wedding.

Tilly was charged but acquitted as Eric refused to testify.

Despite the rocky beginning, they were married for thirteen years before Eric died of cancer.

Tilly Devine was regarded as one of Sydney's wealthiest women throughout the 1920s, 1930s and 1940s, but the Taxation Department assessed her as owing £20,000 in unpaid taxes in 1955. This brought her close to bankruptcy, but she survived and although not as successful thereafter, continued her criminal business empire until she died in 1970 having sold her last brothel two years before.

Queen of Sly-Grog

Kate Leigh was also extremely wealthy, contesting Tilly Devine for the title of Sydney's richest woman.

Known for her violent nature, she shot and killed Snowy Prendergast in 1930 when he and his mates broke into Kate's Riley Street home hoping to relieve her of some of her wealth. She wasn't indicted for the murder. She also disposed of Joseph McNamara, again by shooting.

Her criminal career included being charged 107 times and serving thirteen prison sentences.

During the 1920s and 1930s she owned and operated over 30 sly-grog shops.

As with Tilly Devine, the Taxation Department caught up with her in the mid-1950s and she was declared bankrupt.

At the time of Kate's death she was living in poverty in a one-room apartment over her nephew's shop in Surry Hills.

PHIL THE JEW

Phil Jeffs survived the volatile years of the 1920s and 1930s pretty much unscathed. His sly-grog establishment the *50-50 Club* in Darlinghurst remained one of the most popular spots to enjoy an after-hours tipple.

Although the police raided him regularly he only paid £185 in fines over a two-year period from 1933 to 1935. The cost of licensing in a normal pub was much more expensive.

Phil's other club, the *400*, was established for a higher-class clientele. He brought in a society doctor as a partner to attract the posh types. This partnership was dissolved when after a disagreement Jeffs beat the poor doctor to within an inch of his life and told him to never come back.

Jeffs' wealth grew and he purchased *Oyster Bill's Club* at Tom Ugly's Bridge. After extensive renovations *Oyster Bill's* became one of the most popular venues for Sydneysiders to visit on weekends.

Jeffs was estimated to have accumulated a fortune exceeding £250,000 but he decided to get out of the game. He sold his clubs and retired to a luxury apartment block he had constructed at Ettalong.

Phil Jeffs' Apartment

Jeffs' life became one of luxury and decadence. He accumulated over 2000 books for his library and attracted a bevy of beautiful women whom he showered with gifts.

In October 1945 Phil Jeffs died. Estimates put his wealth at £500,000 but his estate was officially valued at £65,000. Rumour had it the majority of his wealth went to the beautiful women who attended his traditional Jewish funeral.

MELBOURNE:
HOME OF SQUIZZY TAYLOR

Joseph Leslie Theodore Taylor was born in the usual way at Brighton Hospital; the same hospital as the author of this book. The date was June 29th, 1888, and he was born into a respectable family as the second youngest of an eventual five children.

The family lived in Brighton, a leafy middle-class suburb up until 1893 when the depression had a major effect on the family's lives.

This severe economic depression caused the closure and collapse of many banks. The Federal Bank of Australia ran out of money and closed. In August 1893, the Commercial Bank of Australia suspended operations. Twelve other banks soon followed. Those who had put their savings into building societies, as well as those who had borrowed heavily to fund their own speculative investments, found themselves in desperate straits. The depression forced the Taylors to leave Brighton and move to the much less salubrious suburb of Richmond.

Joseph wasn't the smartest kid in the class at Richmond Central, but he wasn't far from it. He gradually lost interest in English and arithmetic and began to spend more time at the racing stables than at school. He found work with Mr Miller the trainer who recognised young Joseph's potential as an apprentice jockey. Although Taylor demonstrated skill in his riding he began to build a reputation of being crooked.

Joseph started to get a lust for easy money, thieving and breaking and entering. His police record began to grow after his first conviction for assault when he was eighteen.

Soon after he was arrested while departing Bendigo for Melbourne, accused of stealing a gold breast pin from a Chinese shopkeeper.

The magistrate found him guilty, fining him £2, or seven days in default.

Squizzy, as he was now called, decided crime was more lucrative if conducted in a group environment, i.e. a gang. He decided he should approach Percy Ramage, the gang leader of the Bourke Street Rats. Percy was famous for his assaults on policemen. He had served six years in gaol for assault.

Percy Ramage

Percy also resided in Richmond. His local pub was the *Spread Eagle Hotel*, located on the corner of Bridge Road and Coppin Street. The hotel first opened its doors in 1854. Most days, members of the Bourke Street Rats could be found swilling their beer at the front bar before being ejected at 6 pm.

Squizzy walked in at 5 pm and ordered a beer from the buxom barmaid.

'Tell me, darling, can you point out Percy Ramage to me?'

'Percy doesn't like being approached by people he doesn't know.'

'My reason to meet him is honourable, love. Will this fiver help you change your mind?'

'All right, I'll have a word with him.'

'I'll wait here at the bar, darling.'

The barmaid made her way to the back of the public bar and approached Percy with Squizzy's request for a meeting. Squizzy could see a man who he thought must be Percy look his way and say something to the barmaid. She returned to where Squizzy was standing drinking his beer.

'Okay, he'll meet with you but first one of his men will pat you down. You'd better not be carrying a weapon.'

'I'm clean sweetie, no worries.'

The little would-be gangster approached the gang leader and one of his men patted him down thoroughly before giving him the all-clear.

'So what the fuck do you want, whoever you are?'

'My name is Squizzy Taylor, Percy, I would be very interested in joining your gang.'

'Would you now and what makes you think I would be interested in you joining us?'

'I'm smart, I can fight, and I've been arrested several times.'

'What were you arrested for?'

'Mainly stealing but I have one assault charge against my name.'

'All right I'll give you a trial and see how you go.'

Squizzy proved himself and after two weeks he was accepted into The Bourke Street Rats.

Squizzy's modus operandi with the gang was pickpocketing. Bourke Street in the 1920s was filled with theatres and fancy restaurants. As the patrons spilled out of the venues, Squizzy would move among them stealing wallets and watches. Percy was well pleased with his new recruit's work.

After twelve months with the gang, Squizzy decided to branch out, forming his own gang.

Taylor established a network of informants who would make him aware of opportunities. These people on the fringe of crime would be paid what Squizzy called a commission.

One such opportunity involved a commercial traveller, Arthur Trotter, employed by MacRobertson's chocolates famous for their Cherry Ripe. He would collect money from resellers such as milk bars and hold it overnight. His usual practice was to stow the money away under his mattress in a leather bag and take it into the office the following morning.

Two of Squizzy's men overhead Arthur boasting about sleeping on a small fortune while he was drinking at the *Fitzroy Arms Hotel.*

It was a stinking hot night in Melbourne and the temperature was still 90 degrees at 9 pm.

Arthur had had a successful day collecting £215, which he brought home to his house in Fitzroy.

He entered through the back door, greeting his wife Beatrice and his young son Tom.

'Hello darling did you have a good day?' asked Beatrice.

'I did sweetheart, but it was bloody hot. I can't wait to get out of this suit.'

'I don't blame you. I'll have a cold beer waiting for you. I might even have one for a change seeing it's so hot.'

The young couple sat on the back step sipping their beers and playing with Tom.

'Right, it's time for tea. We're having sausages and salad.'

'Sounds good to me, darl.'

After tea, they listened to the radio for an hour or so then Arthur began reconciling the accounts, and Beatrice retired to bed.

It was about one in the morning and Arthur and Beatrice were both in a deep sleep when they were woken by the light in their bedroom coming on. Startled, they sat up in bed to see two masked men holding revolvers. One was tall and the other had the frame of a jockey.

'What do you want?' asked Arthur.

'We want the money bag.'

'That's the boss's. You can't have that.'

'For God's sake, Arthur, give them the money,' cried Beatrice.

'Okay, let me get it for you.'

Trotter got out of bed, pretending to retrieve the moneybag. Instead he lashed out at the taller bandit but failed to land the punch. The bandit shot Arthur Trotter in the eye.

Trotter collapsed on the floor. Beatrice and Tommy were screaming. The jockey ignored the mayhem, snatching the bag from under the mattress and fleeing.

A neighbour heard the shot and the screaming and called the police.

Arthur was raced to hospital but died soon after arrival.

The police arrived in force, eight in all, and they searched the Trotter residence with a fine toothcomb looking for evidence. They thought they had found something of significance in two sets of fingerprints on the windowsill. They were disappointed when the prints turned out to belong to one of the constables.

The police were encouraged when they discovered another set of handprints on another windowsill. The handprint had a distinctive scar on an index finger. A photograph was taken and distributed to police forces in all states. The investigation was in luck. The prints belonged to Harold Thomson, a big man who was a member of Squizzy Taylor's gang. He fitted the description given by Beatrice Trotter.

Several police officers broke into a cottage in Jones Lane, off Little Lonsdale Street, and arrested Thompson.

His girlfriend Flossie assured the police he was home on the night of the killing.

Squizzy, who never spoke throughout the home invasion, was not arrested.

When Thompson went to trial his defence lawyer provided proof that the fingerprints found in the Trotter house did not match the prints taken while his client resided in gaol. The other issue was that Mrs Trotter couldn't positively identify Thompson as the man who shot and killed her husband.

The jury acquitted Thompson.

Taxi

Bob Burns had owned and operated Globe Motor Taxis for a good many years and he expected this day to be no different than any other. When the telephone rang he answered it in the usual way.

'Globe Motor Taxis, can I help you?'

A gruff voice on the other end of the line spoke.

'I want a limousine tomorrow morning from eight to one o'clock.'

'Yes, sir, I'm sure we can help you with that.'

'How much is it going to set me back?'

'We charge a shilling a mile and five shillings an hour waiting time.'

'What car will you be providing? I want a bloody good one.'

'A Unic. It's very comfortable and extremely reliable.'

'Good. It's essential I get back by one o'clock as I have further business to attend to.'

Unic

'May I ask you your name, sir?'

'L'Estrange.'

'And what address to pick you up?'

'Cliveden Mansions, 192 Wellington Parade, East Melbourne.'

'And where do you wish to be driven to?'

'Eltham.'

Mr L'Estrange then hung up.

The following morning, Bill Haines, one of the company's best young drivers, reported for his shift. Bob Burns assigned him the L'Estrange job. Haines checked the motor vehicle and then headed off to Cliveden Mansions to collect his passengers.

Bill drove the Unic to the Cliveden Mansions and as he arrived at the prestigious address he noticed two men standing on the footpath. One was a large fellow and the other a short skinny one. They waved to him and so he parked the car.

'Good morning. Mr L'Estrange, I presume?'

'That's right.'

The two men got into the back seat, and they began their journey.

'Right, driver, this is what's going to happen. You're going to drive us out to Eltham where we will intercept a bloke on a bicycle. He's a bank manager and he'll have a bag of money. The chances are he won't give it up easily which means we'll have to shoot him. Are you okay with that?'

'No, it's not all right with me. You're asking me to be an accessory to murder. I have a mind to inform the police of your plan.'

'Fair enough— it doesn't hurt to ask. Park the car and we'll get out.'

The two men looked at each other. Squizzy nodded to his partner who took out his pistol and shot the unsuspecting driver twice in the back of the head.

Bill Haines died instantly.

Squizzy and Williamson vacated the car and ran up Bulleen Road, leaving the blood-soaked Unic behind.

The car remained parked on the side of the road for over two hours before a delivery van driver, Albert Mills, discovered poor Haines. Mills notified the police who arrived within the hour.

Detective Sergeant Bannon was placed in charge of the case. He discovered that Hubert De Mole was the bank manager the gangsters had in their sights. He had £400 in his bag; a sizeable amount.

There were several witnesses who identified Squizzy and Williamson running from the scene of the crime. On March 9th the two gangsters were arrested on the charge of murder.

They both appeared in court in April 1916 before Justice Hood and a jury.

Both men had alibis that seemed credible to the jury members. The prosecution witnesses seemed less so. After several hours of deliberating the jury found the defendants not guilty.

Fitzroy Vendetta

Chapter 25

VENDETTA FLAMES OUT AGAIN.
MEN KILLED, A WOMAN HURT

Squizzy Taylor Invades Enemy in Carlton House
in Gun Duel Shoots Him and Wounds His Mot[...]

THEN STAGGERS OUT, COLLAPSES, D[...]

TWO men, both notorious members of the underworld, were shot dead, and a w[...]
wounded, last night in a desperate revolver duel in a bedroom in a house in B[...]
street, Carlton.

THE shooting was the outcome of a vendetta, which had existed between the dead[...]
for some years. Although the associates of the men are reticent as to what led[...]
the shooting, the detectives believe rivalry for the affections of a woman was the imme[...]
incentive.

The Victims are:— **DEAD**
LESLIE (SQUIZZY) TAYLOR, 42, of Darlington-parade, Richmond. Bullet w[...]
in right side over the lungs.
JOHN (SNOWY) CUTMORE, 35, of Barkly-street, Carlton. Bullet wound over [...]
and on little finger of right hand.

WOUNDED
BRIDGET CUTMORE, 56, mother of John Cutmore. Shot through right sho[...]
Condition not serious.

The Sailors Arms Hotel

Squizzy met up with his arch-rival Henry Stokes at *The Sailors Arms Hotel* in Fitzroy. Stokes led the Fitzroy Gang. Squizzy now lived in Richmond and was known as the boss of the Richmond Gang. They decided to join forces and rob Kilpatrick's, the biggest jewellery store in Melbourne. The plan was for Mathew Daly, one of Squizzy's lads, to purchase a wedding present from the jewellery store.

'Good afternoon sir how can I help you?' asked the salesman, Henry Harbinson.

'I'm looking for a nice present for my niece. She's getting married next Saturday.'

'Well, sir, I'm sure we will be able to help you. How much were you thinking of spending?'

'I thought about £5 should do it.'

'Excellent. May I suggest this muffineer in sterling silver?'

'Yes, I think that would be suitable. I will need to pay a £1 deposit and return with the balance when I withdraw money from my bank.'

'Certainly sir I'll place the muffineer out the back of the store ready for your return.'

Daly returned to the store at 1.30 pm and paid the balance to Harbinson. A half an hour later he returned again telling the salesman that his wife didn't think the present chosen was good enough.

'My wife has suggested a pair of superior cruets. Do you have something that might suit?'

'Yes, I'm sure we have something that would satisfy your wife.'

Harbinson unlocked three glass sliding doors, reaching in to show Daley four different sets. He chose one and handed the salesman a £10 note.

'I'll have to get you some change from the back of the store, sir; I won't be long.'

As soon as Harbinson turned to walk to the rear of the store Daley slid two of the panels open and took two trays of the finest diamond rings on display.

When the salesman returned with the change he was surprised to find his customer had disappeared. In his place was a swarthy man in a dark coat and black felt hat placing a thick chain through the outside door handles. A large brass padlock had been used to fasten it. He and all the other staff were effectively prisoners.

The gang had got away with £2,000 worth of rings. The police suspected Squizzy but had no proof.

Squizzy, Daly and Frank Jones represented the Richmond Gang while Henry, Ted Whiting and Long Harry Slater comprised the Fitzroy Gang.

The robbery went well, but the three Fitzroy boys were identified and later arrested. The remainder of the Fitzroy Gang became suspicious that someone from the Richmond Gang had tipped off the police. Their suspicion increased when Frank from the Richmond Gang became a prosecution witness in exchange for immunity.

The three men were found not guilty, but outside the court, a brawl broke out and Squizzy was badly beaten.

'Hey, Taylor, I suppose you're disappointed we got off,' shouted Ted Whiting.

'Not at all, Ted. I'm delighted you beat the rap.'

'Yeah, so how come one of your own turned prosecution witness?'

'He was just saving his own arse, mate. It wasn't anything personal.'

'I don't believe it you little turd.'

One of the Fitzroy Gang hit Squizzy over the head with a baton and began to kick him while he was on the ground, fracturing Squizzy's right leg. The Fitzroy boys took off down the street. The Fitzroy Vendetta had begun.

Squizzy Recovering After His Beating

Attack and counter-attack occurred for some time. Many were injured but nobody got killed.

The Melbourne newspapers reported each incident, yet no charges were laid due to members of each gang refusing to testify.

'Ted, I'm fucking sure Squizzy ripped us off. There's no fucking way we got our fair share from the Kilpatrick's robbery.'

'I'm with you, Harry. I reckon we should confront the evil dwarf and get him to hand over our fair share.'

February 19th, 1919

'Squizzy, love, can I ask you to zip me up?'

'I'd rather zip you down, Dolly. You look smashing tonight.'

'We don't have time for that, darling. We'll be late for the party. Maybe if we're not too tired when we get home.'

'Yeah, I suppose you're right, sweetie. It's just that I'm not really looking forward to tonight what with the Fitzroy boys being there and all.'

'Don't worry, Squizzy, just ignore them. There will be lots of other people we know.'

Squizzy and Dolly caught a taxi from their Richmond home to where the party was being held in Fitzroy. Squizzy knocked on the front door and Percy Hargraves let them in.

'G'day Squizzy, I haven't seen you since you moved over to Richmond. Who's this delightful young thing you have on your arm?'

'Percy, please meet my wife, Dolly. Darling, this is Percy Hargraves. We go back a long way.'

'Pleased to meet you, Dolly. Come on and I'll get you both a drink. What would you like?'

'I'd like a gin and tonic please, Percy.'

'Just a beer for me mate.'

Percy disappeared into the kitchen to organise the Taylors' drinks.

As he was mixing Dolly's G&T one of his mates from the Fitzroy Gang, Ted Whiting, approached him.

'Percy, whack this powder into Dolly's drink. She'll be out like a light before she knows it.'

'Why in the hell would I want to do that, Ted?'

'Mate, take a look what she's got hanging around her neck. It's from the Kilpatrick job, I'm sure of it. Squizzy ripped us off. There's no fucking way we received our fair share. We pinch her necklace and we'll be square.'

Ted's plan went without a hitch. Dolly complained of feeling woozy. Ted's wife Doreen suggested she might wish to lie down in the main bedroom for a little while.

Dolly was out to it as soon as she hit the bed. Her £250 necklace was removed and apart from some molestation from one of the other gang members she woke reasonably unscathed an hour later.

Squizzy was none the wiser as he was in the backyard holding council with some of his gang members.

Neither Dolly nor Squizzy noticed the necklace gone until they arrived back in their Richmond home.

'I needed to lie down for a short while, love. It may have come off in the bed.'

'I'll call on Ted tomorrow and see if we can find it. I hope we can. I went to a lot of trouble to get that for you.'

Squizzy telephoned Ted Whiting the next morning, explaining how the necklace had gone missing.

'Squizzy, don't bother coming around, mate. We'll search the place high and low. If it's here we'll find it. I'll let you know.'

'Okay, Ted, I'll wait for your call. Dolly's very upset as you would imagine.'

The next morning Ted called Squizzy with the bad news.

'I'm sorry, mate; we searched everywhere and couldn't find the thing. Maybe some bastard nicked it when your Mrs was laying down.'

Squizzy didn't believe his adversary one little bit. He suspected the Fitzroy Gang had planned all along to rob Dolly of her necklace.

Ted Whiting

Squizzy called a meeting of his most trusted gang members. The purpose of the meeting was to plan the home invasion and shooting of Ted Whiting in revenge for the robbery of Dolly's necklace.

'Right lads, I'll take three of you when we get the bastard. You'll be armed with a pistol but unless there's a problem I'll do the shooting. Is that clear?'

'Yes, boss.'

'We go tomorrow night; the address is 16 Webb Street Fitzroy. I want you here at 10 pm so we surprise the prick when he's in bed.

'Yes, boss.'

Harry Jones, John Thompson and Robert Francis were all waiting on the footpath in front of Squizzy Taylor's house. Parked on the street was Squizzy's Oldsmobile. Squizzy opened his front door with a Gladstone bag in his right hand.

'Get in lads, let's get going.'

As Squizzy drove, he instructed Harry to open the bag and distribute the weaponry to the other passengers. The drive took only thirty minutes as the traffic was light, so they arrived at Webb Street at 10.30 pm.

'As agreed we all move to the side of the house where Ted and his wife's bedroom is situated. Rob, you smash the window and get in first. I'll follow you. If he's armed shoot the prick but if not leave him to me. Everybody understand?'

Rob smashed the window with a baseball bat and clambered inside. He yelled at the stunned couple not to move.

Squizzy was next to enter. He stood at the end of the bed and fired six times into the ex-boxer's head.

Ted's wife lay there screaming.

No bastard could survive that, thought Taylor.

The four gangsters departed via the front door, speeding away to their Richmond sanctuary.

Nobody was ever charged with the attempted murder. Ted Whiting survived the assassination attempt and refused to testify against Squizzy Taylor.

MAY 1919

Not long after the Whiting shooting, Harold Pendlebury, one of Squizzy's Richmond Gang, was walking along Bridge Road when a car pulled up beside him. An unknown person, likely to be a member of the Fitzroy Gang, shot Pendlebury seven times leaving him to bleed to death on the footpath.

A Good Samaritan drove the gangster to the hospital where doctors removed the bullets, saving his life.

The Fitzroy Vendetta continued.

Robbie Hargraves from the Richmond Gang was enjoying a quiet ale in *The Spread Eagle Hotel* when two members of the Fitzroy Gang entered, making a beeline for Robbie. They grabbed him by the neck and dragged him out of the pub and into an alleyway, which ran beside the hotel. They punched and kicked him to within an inch of his life, leaving him bleeding on the bluestone pavers. When Robbie regained consciousness he crawled back into the bar where the barman called an ambulance. Despite his horrendous injuries Robbie lived to fight another day.

Squizzy and two of his gang members were drinking whisky at the kitchen table in the Taylors' Richmond house.

Squizzy's House

'What are we going to do about these Fitzroy pricks, boss?'

'Well, I can tell you now these bastards aren't getting away with it. I have on good advice that Whiting and a couple of his Fitzroy mates will be playing poker at Jimmie Black's place tonight. I suggest we pay them a little visit.'

Squizzy instructed the other two gang members to bring their Colt 45s while he carried his new pride and joy, a Tommy Gun capable of firing 1500 rounds per minute.

The gang of three drove to Black's address in Napier Street, Fitzroy. Squizzy leant out of the passenger side window and fired off a full magazine, 100 rounds in all, in just over four seconds. He knew they would be playing their game in the front parlour and therefore he figured there would be four bodies on the floor.

'Quick, let's get out of here fast before the cops arrive,' yelled Taylor.

The car sped off, heading for Squizzy's home in Richmond where they planned to play poker themselves in case the police turned up. The guns were dropped off on the way at another gang member's house.

What Squizzy and the boys didn't know was the four poker players were having a break and pouring themselves a whisky in the kitchen at the rear of the house.

No one was injured; just extremely upset.

The vendetta continued throughout 1919 with shootings and bashings taking place on a regular basis. As 1920 began the violence subsided. Whiting was serving a prison sentence and Slater and Thorpe had moved to Sydney.

Not only did the vendetta end but so did Squizzy's first marriage. He married Lorna Kelly on the 19th of May 1920.

HIDE AND SEEK

Squizzy remained active in the Melbourne crime scene throughout 1920 - 1921, performing a series of burglaries.

His most provocative activity was robbing the Commercial Bank in Thornbury of £323. As usual, he was found not guilty when brought to trial.

JUNE 10, 1921

Squizzy called a meeting with two of his gang members; the purpose was to plan a robbery on a bonded warehouse in Melbourne Central.

'Fellas, we're going to hit Scales Warehouse. The place is stacked to the rafters with furs.'

'What sort of furs, Squizzy?'

'Fucking mink, mate. We'll be able to sell them for a fortune.'

'Sounds good. When do we go?'

'Tomorrow night. Let's meet at the *Queen's Arms* in King Street.'

'Done, see you there, Squizzy.'

'Not so quickly— we need to pinch a truck to load the booty.'

'I know where there's a beauty, Squizzy. She'd be perfect for the job.'

'Beauty Jack, go and get it and don't get caught. I don't want to lose you or the fucking truck.'

'She'll be right, Squizzy. I'll bring her around the back of Scales about midnight.'

The gang of four waited outside the King Street warehouse until Jack arrived with the truck. It was exactly what Squizzy had hoped for; a furniture removal van.

John Olsen used bolt cutters to cut the chain on the gate and Jack drove the van in, backing it close the large wooden doors.

Squizzy's specialist lock picker, Frank Pascale, took only five minutes to crack the lock.

They opened the doors and Jack drove into the vast warehouse.

'Okay, boys, apparently the furs are stored at the end of row three. Let's go and get them.'

The gang took over an hour to load the furs into the van. Finally, the last fur was loaded. Squizzy and Jack sat in the cabin and the other gang members hopped in the back.

'Right Jack, let's get the fuck out of here.'

Jack drove the van out of the warehouse, but there was something wrong. The gates had been closed and a new lock attached. Squizzy saw several flashlights shining into the cabin.

'Stop! This is the police. You're all under arrest.'

Six policemen appeared with batons drawn. Squizzy knew the game was up and he and his gang surrendered to the constabulary.

Squizzy was charged with breaking and entering. The magistrate released him on £600 bail.

The trial date arrived but Squizzy didn't. He forfeited his bail. The elusive Squizzy Taylor was not seen for another twelve months.

The Getaway Truck

WHILE THE CAT'S AWAY

CHAPTER 27

While Squizzy was holed up in his East Melbourne flat safe from Victoria's finest, things on the street began to get ugly again.

A notorious member of the Fitzroy Gang, Joseph Cotter, decided to pay one of Squizzy's gambling clubs a visit. He used his Tommy Gun to spray the Bourke Street establishment with bullets injuring one of the staff, a barman.

OCTOBER 1921
ASCOT RACECOURSE

Joe Cotter decided to attend the races for some relaxation. After all, he'd been very busy shooting people, mostly members of Squizzy Taylor's gang.

He approached his favourite bookmaker, Long John West.

'G'day John, are you winning or losing, mate?'

'Not having a very good day, Joe, but now that you're here things might change.'

'Don't bet on it you cheeky bastard.'

'So what's your fancy for the fifth, Joe?'

'I like the sound of Fleet of Foot. What are you paying?'

'It's £2.50 the win and £1.0 the place.'

'All right. I'll place £50 on the nose thanks, mate.'

'You got it.'

John handed the betting slip to Joe. The gambler headed for the bar for a quick whisky before the race.

Standing next to him at the bar was his archenemy, John Olsen.

'Well, I'll be fucked! If it isn't the drongo from Fitzroy.'

'Who are you calling a drongo, you fat prick?'

Without warning, Joe hit Olsen square on the nose, making it bleed.

'You broke my fucking nose, you bastard!'

It became a free for all as others aligned the two factions joined the fray. It wasn't until the police arrived that the donnybrook was broken up.

Both Cotter and Olsen were evicted from the racetrack.

Ironically Fleet of Foot won the fifth, and Joe returned to Ascot the following week to collect his winnings.

Cotter was known to hold a grudge and soon after the racetrack fight he stalked and shot John Olsen in Fitzroy. He was arrested and went to trial, but the jury found him not guilty on the grounds of self-defence.

In the meantime, Squizzy was still underground, keeping his head low in the East Melbourne flat. His new girlfriend, Ida *Babe* Pender, began to complain that she had no new clothes and even if she did they weren't able to go out anywhere.

Ida Babe Pender

'Fucking hell Rob, Ida is giving me a hard time about not having any new clobber to wear. I think I'm going to have to get her some to shut her up,' said Squizzy.

'What, go and buy her a new wardrobe?' asked Rob Livingstone.

'Fuck no! I'm not going to buy anything. I mean to nick it. Rob, I want you to find a shop with nice clothes that we can knock over.'

'Okay, boss. I'll see what I can find.'

Rob found a boutique in Elsternwick which fitted the bill, and he reported back to his boss.

'I found a shop which will be perfect. They've got nice clothes and there's a laneway at the back so it will be easy to steal the stuff and get away.'

'That sounds ideal. We'll make it next Monday when it should be pretty quiet.'

When Monday arrived, Squizzy, Rob and another member of the gang, Harry, broke into the shop and gathered as many clothes as they could. The getaway car was to be driven by Phil Case with Ida in the passenger's seat.

Unfortunately, just as Squizzy, Rob and Harry were heading for the car, a police car turned into the laneway.

The sight of three blokes carrying women's clothing made the officers suspicious. The chase was on through the streets of Elsternwick and St Kilda.

Eventually Squizzy and the gang lost the cops, and they made their way back to Squizzy's flat.

'Darling, these clothes are exquisite, thank you.'

'Nothing is too good for my Ida. Why don't you try on a few dresses and show me how beautiful you look?'

'I'd rather take this dress off and show you how I look, sweetheart.'

'Now you're talking, babe.'

The next day the police raided Ida's flat as well as the houses of Rob and Harry. Squizzy eluded the police yet again.

Ida Pender turned police witness and was housed in a safe house but mysteriously disappeared. Without Ida's testimony, a conviction for breaking and entering against Rob and Harry could not be proved. The elusive Squizzy could not be found.

Thomas Berriman was the accountant at the Hawthorn Branch of the Commercial Bank. He was liked by his customers and staff and was known to tell a joke or two. His staff would politely laugh although the jokes he told were more often than not corny.

'Mr Hathaway, I need to deliver this suitcase to head office. I shouldn't be more than a couple of hours. Could you keep an eye on things while I'm gone please?'

'Yes, certainly, Mr Berriman. Is there anything I should be aware of?'

'No, it should be a quiet morning.'

What nobody, including Mr Hathaway knew—or so Berriman believed— was that the case was filled with £ notes; £1,851 in all.

The bank manager walked briskly to Glenferrie Station. He expected no trouble, but trouble was what he got.

'Hello, Mr Berriman nice morning for a walk,' said a stranger.

Berriman thought this man must be a bank customer he was not familiar with.

'Yes, it is,' he agreed. 'Mores the pity, I have to catch a train.'

'That suitcase looks heavy, Mr Berriman. Let me carry it for you. Give yourself a break.'

'No, I'm fine, thank you.'

'I think you may have misunderstood me. What I meant was give me the fucking suitcase.'

'I certainly will not. Get out of my way. I have a train to catch.'

Another man similarly attired walked up to the defiant bank manager, pulled out a pistol and fired three shots into Berriman's chest. The men grabbed the suitcase and ran to a waiting car, speeding off down Glenferrie Road.

A witness called for an ambulance which arrived within fifteen minutes, but Berriman died in hospital.

Several witnesses were able to identify the murderers from police mug shots. Richard Buckley and Angus Murray, an escaped convict, were identified, enabling the police to raid a house in Barkly Street, St Kilda a few days after the robbery. Arrested were Squizzy Taylor, Ida Pender, and Murray.

They were escorted to the St Kilda watch-house where Sergeant Bill Armstrong interrogated Squizzy.

'Right Taylor, this robbery and shooting has your name all over it.'

'I'm innocent, sergeant, I assure you I wasn't there at the time of the robbery.'

'You may not have been there, but I'll bet my balls you planned and directed it.'

'No, sarge, you've got it all wrong. I had no idea what was going on. I was home reading a good book.'

'I'm surprised you know how to read, Squizzy. What book are you reading?'

'*Little Women.*'

'Really.'

'Really.'

'I'm arresting you, Taylor, for "Being the occupier of a house frequented by thieves." You are also charged with harbouring an escaped convict.'

The following morning Sergeant Armstrong became aware that Berriman had died overnight in hospital. Things had got more serious. Murray was charged with murder and Squizzy was charged as an accessory.

Buckley eluded the police despite several raids and appeals for public assistance. Finally, a reward of £500 was offered without a result.

Squizzy and Murray faced the court alone. The coroner, after a lengthy inquest into Berriman's death, returned a verdict of wilful murder by Buckley and Murray with Squizzy Taylor as an accessory.

Squizzy, after several appeals, was granted bail and immediately contacted several witnesses all of whom were threatened with violence of the most intense nature if they testified against him.

He also devised a plan to break Murray out from prison. This involved bribing a warder and using sheets tied together to scale down the prison wall. The plan failed Taylor and his accomplices were charged with conspiring to enable an escape from Melbourne Gaol.

Murray was tried and convicted of Berriman's murder and sentenced to hang despite the fact it was Buckley who pulled the trigger.

Despite several appeals and a huge public protest, he was hanged on 14 April 1924. Over two thousand protestors demonstrated outside the prison walls on the morning of his execution.

The police didn't give up on finding Buckley. Following up on a tip they tracked him down in a house in Moonee Ponds seven years after Murray's execution.

He was finally brought to trial and convicted. He was sentenced to hang but this sentence was commuted to life in prison. In 1946 he was released, enabling him to die with his family by his side.

OCTOBER 26, 1927

The last of Bruhn's inner circle, Snowy Cutmore, decided to return to his hometown of Melbourne in October 1927. Snowy was a member of the Fitzroy Gang and his hatred for Squizzy dated back to the Fitzroy Vendetta.

His good mate Herbert Wilson joined Snowy and his wife.

Cutmore had lost none of the hate he held for Squizzy Taylor during his time in Sydney. As soon as he arrived back in Melbourne he began to badmouth his old adversary.

Cutmore continued to drink heavily, becoming obnoxious to the extreme. After an all-day drinking session with Wilson at the Richmond racecourse, Cutmore fell ill with influenza and was confined to bed at his mother's house in Carlton.

Cutmore was lying in bed and his mother was cooking his favourite meal, lamb roast, the smell of which wafted into his bedroom.

A loud knock on the front door alerted him.

'Good evening, Mrs Cutmore. My name is Squizzy Taylor. I'm a close friend of your son's. May I have a quick word with him please?'

'Yes, certainly, his room is the second on the left.'

Squizzy drew his Colt from under his coat and quietly entered Cutmore's room.

'Hello Snowy, feeling a bit the worse for wear?'

'What the fuck do you want?'

'Not much. Just the front pew at your fucking funeral.'

Squizzy pointed his revolver at the bedridden gangster and fired a single shot, hitting Cutmore in the left shoulder. Unbeknownst to Squizzy, Snowy had a gun under his pillow. He grabbed it and shot Squizzy in the chest. A flurry of shots ensued, twelve in all.

At the end of the shootout, Snowy Cutmore lay dead. His mother received a wound when she ran into the room. Squizzy staggered out of the house, managing to get to the hospital where he died soon after.

Neighbours called the police who arrived not long after the shooting. They found Cutmore in bed riddled with bullets.

Friday 28th October 1927:

Suspicious Death Of Squizzy Taylor

-Joseph 'Squizzy' Taylor, aged 43, one of Australia's most notorious criminals, was gunned down in a house in the Melbourne suburb of Carlton yesterday evening. A gun battle occurred between Taylor and another known criminal, 'Snowy' Cutmore, who was also killed. Police alledging each shot the other over a long standing fued.

Sydney and Melbourne were not the only cities that spawned gangsters and whores in the 1920s.

America became a hot bed of organised crime.

DRY AS A DEAD DINGO'S DONGA
THE AGE OF PROHIBITION

CHAPTER 28

JANUARY 17TH, 1920
UNITED STATES OF AMERICA

The 18th amendment prohibiting the consumption, manufacture and transportation of intoxicating liquors came into effect. This period was known as Prohibition.

The temperance movement had lobbied hard since the mid-1850s to prohibit alcohol. The movement based their argument on Benjamin Rush's *An Inquiry Into the Effects of Ardent Spirits Upon the Human Body and Mind.*

The Volstead Act was passed by both Congress and the Senate, giving police widespread powers to enforce the law, but the illegal production known as bootlegging and the widespread proliferation of speakeasies together with the rapid rise of gangs and associated violence made Prohibition unenforceable.

THE DRUNKARDS PROGRESS.

GANGSTERS
AL CAPONE

Al Capone became the most infamous gangster of the Prohibition period considered as "Public Enemy Number One". Capone became very wealthy from his life of crime— in one year alone he made $100 million, but he was convicted of tax evasion and died in Alcatraz.

LUCKY LUCIANO

Lucky imported Scotch whisky from Scotland and Canada and rum from the Caribbean.

He accumulated more wealth than Al Capone, allowing him to live a life of privilege. After Prohibition, he established a prostitution ring, which became the largest in America. This led to his conviction and incarceration.

MEYER LANSKY

Meyer was known to head the most violent gang of the era along with his partner in crime Bugsy Siegal.

JOHNNY TORRIO

Torrio was the founder of the crime empire that Al Capone took over. Torrio saw the potential of smuggling booze early in the Prohibition era. His then boss refused to get involved so Johnny murdered him.

Johnny Torrio is considered a founder of organised crime in America.

BUGS MORAN

Bugs was the arch-rival of Al Capone and Johnny Torrio. He is known to have murdered Capone's associates to solidify his position in the underworld.

MACHINE GUN KELLY

Machine Gun Kelly was born as George Kelly Barnes in Memphis Tennessee in 1895.

He worked as a bootlegger during the Prohibition era, supplying grog to speakeasies and various private clients.

He began his adult live innocently enough when he attended Mississippi State College studying agriculture. However, he began to get into trouble with the faculty staff and dropped out. He met Geneva Ramsey at college. She too dropped out of her course, and they married. George found work as a cab driver and then several other jobs, none of which he could hold down.

The instability in his work life led him to become a bootlegger at the age of nineteen. Being in an illegal profession meant young George was arrested seven times.

George started to mix with gangsters who influenced his behaviour and finally Geneva had had enough and divorced him.

He met his second wife, Kathryn Thorne, who shared his criminal intent.

JULY 18, 1925

George arrived home after delivering twelve cases of whisky to a speakeasy downtown.

'I'm home, darling, let's have a drink. It's my birthday— did you remember?'

'Of course, I remembered. Sit down on the couch and I'll bring you a scotch.'

'That sounds like a great idea.'

Kathryn brought her husband his drink and went back to the kitchen to retrieve his birthday present.

'Happy birthday, darling.'

She presented George with a long box wrapped in striped paper, tied with ribbon and a large bow.

'Gee, what could this be?'

'Well, you'd better open it and see, George.'

George ripped open the paper and took the lid off the box. He didn't say a word. He just stared at it.

'So, what do you think? Do you like it?'

'I love it, babe! I just can't believe you've given me such a wonderful birthday present.'

George gently lifted it out of the box, cradling it in his hands.

George had received a brand-new Tommy Gun. He could now assert his authority. From that day he became known as Machine Gun Kelly.

'Tell me, gorgeous— have you ever used a Tommy Gun before?'

'I have to admit I haven't. I've used Colts and shotguns but nothing like this little beauty.'

'Well, what we need to do is take it out into the woods where you can practise shooting targets. Once you've perfected it we can decide how we can make some real money out of it.'

The following day, George and Kathryn drove out to Lebanon Hills Regional Park in Apple Valley. The 1869 acres were perfectly suited for an improvised firing range.

They walked two miles from the car park until they found an open area surrounded by tall trees.

'I'll pin this target to a tree, babe. Do your best to hit it.'

George took aim at the target and pulled the trigger. The recoil surprised him as did the thirty bullets it fired in less than a minute. His accuracy was atrocious.

'You're going to have to do better than that, George. You missed the fucking target altogether.'

'It's not that easy, Kate. If you think it is, you try it.'

Kate took the gun from her husband and took up a firing position, aiming for the bull's eye. She slowly pulled the trigger. Ten of the fifteen bullets hit the target and one pierced the bull's eye.

'There you go sweetie; it's not that difficult. The key is not firing too many shots off at once. You need to have a steady hand.'

The remainder of the afternoon was spent with George mastering the machine gun and by the end of the day he matched Kate's accuracy.

'Right; now we need to plan a job that will earn us some real money.'

They drove home discussing the possibilities.

Kidnapped

George, Kathryn and their close friend Albert Bates were sitting in the Kellys' sitting room discussing their plan to make a stack of money.

'Okay, we've identified our target. This fella Urschel is fucking loaded. All we need to do is grab him out of his home, stick him in a safe house and wait for his grieving family to pay us $200,000. Then we let the fucker go.'

'Sounds like a plan, George. When do we do it?' asked Albert.

'Tomorrow night. He and his wife and some friends will be playing bridge. They'll be concentrating on the cards, so they won't notice us breaking in.'

'We're not grabbing her, are we?'

'No, we'll tie her and her friend up and leave them there to be found. We'll take the two men.'

July 22ND, 1933
Oklahoma City

Walter Jarrett and his wife Lucy arrived at the Urschel mansion at seven pm to partake in their weekly bridge game. They were let in by Charles and offered French champagne, which was gracefully accepted by the couple.

The game had just begun when George, brandishing his Thompson Machine Gun and Albert with a sawn-off shotgun stormed into the room.

Charles Urschel and his wife

'Everybody lie on the floor, do as we say, and no one gets shot. Good, now place your hands behind your backs.'

Albert tied the four petrified bridge players with strong cord.

There they lay with their faces against the carpet.

'What do you intend to do with us?' asked Urschel.

'You'll find out soon enough,' said George. 'Albert, bring the car around to the front. Drive up the driveway. I'll open the garage door to let you in.'

'I didn't think we were going to use our own names.'

'Shit, sorry pal.'

The kidnappers escorted the bound and gagged victims to the garage and pushed them into the trunk. It was fortunate for them the vehicle was an Oldsmobile, and the trunk was large enough for the two men.

The two women remained tied on the floor. Kelly intended to notify the cops anonymously in a few hours.

Kelly and Bates drove the three and a half hours to Paris, Texas, where they intended to stay in an old farmhouse until the ransom was paid.

They pulled the two men out of the trunk. They were in good shape considering the amount of time they spent in such a confined space.

Kelly and Bates escorted them into the house and placed each in a separate room to deny them communication.

'What we need to do is get Urschel to write the ransom note so the bastards can't track us,' said Kelly.

'That sounds like a good plan. Are we still going to demand $200,000?'

'Yeah.'

The kidnappers forced the oilman to write the ransom note demanding $200,000.

A business associate of Urschel came up with the money. What Kelly and Bates were unaware of was that the notes were registered, allowing for easy tracking.

Despite being blindfolded Urschel kept a mental note of the sounds around him, including an aeroplane that flew over at the same time every day.

When he and Jarrett were released, Charles was able to recount his experiences. This helped the police to discover the house and eventually arrest the kidnappers.

Kelly 2nd from left

The kidnapping of Urschel and the two trials that resulted were historic in several ways. They were:

1. The first federal criminal trials in the United States in which film cameras were allowed.
2. The first kidnapping trials after the passage of the so-called Lindberg Law, which made kidnapping a federal crime.
3. The first major case solved by L Edgar Hoover's FBI; and
4. The first prosecution in which defendants were transported by aeroplane.

His gravestone, marked "George B. Kelley".

COCKNEY GANGSTERS

CHAPTER 30

When we think of the roaring twenties and gangsters and moles one tends to relate these concepts to America and the notorious gangsters such as Al Capone, Lucky Luciano and Bugs Malone.

Great Britain also had its fair share of gangsters, all of whom were members of crime gangs such as The Peaky Blinders, The Elephant Boys, and The Birmingham Boys.

THE PEAKY BLINDERS

Thomas Gilbert Gang Leader

Members of the Peaky Blinders

The Peaky Blinders got their name largely from the peaked woollen caps all the members wore. Members of the gang also wore tailored jackets, silk scarves, waistcoats, bell-bottom trousers and leather boots.

A common belief as to how the gang got its name not only referenced their peaked caps but also the practice of sewing razor blades into the peak. The caps became the gang's weapon of choice as they would head-butt their adversary causing temporary blindness. A gentler theory was that Peaky derived from the peaked cap and the Blinders was slang for a dapper appearance. Rumour would have it the former was the more accurate description.

These well-dressed lads stole, ran protection rackets and carried out various other criminal activities around Birmingham in the 1920s and 1930s.

Birmingham in 1920s

BRUMMAGEM BOYS AKA BIRMINGHAM BOYS

This infamous gang, led by Billie Kimber, ruled the racetracks throughout England.

Billie Kimber

This group of dapper gentlemen are not on their way to a church picnic.

They are in fact at Hammersmith Broadway ready to depart for the races at Ascot. Billy Kimber is among this group of notorious gangsters. He is standing in the background (back row, second right). Kimber was the brains behind the Brummagem Gang as well as the brawn. Take note of the gentlemen in peaked caps.

Although this picture depicts a happy and congenial group, within a few months the various gangs represented were involved in a bitter and bloody feud that became known as the 'Racecourse Wars'.

THE ELEPHANT & CASTLE MOB

This mob was one of many gangs operating in London's criminal underworld in 1920s and 1930s. Their partners in crime were the Birmingham Boys led by Billy Kimber.

The gang rivalled north and east London gangs including the notorious Sabini Gang.

Darby Sabini

The Elephant Mob targeted the racecourses where bookies were required to pay the mob protection money. They were also dominant in London's West End evicting rival gangs such as the West End Boys and the Titanic Gang.

Two brothers, Wag and Wal, took over the leadership of the gang, battling their much-hated rival Sabini for control of allocation pitches on racecourses and protection for bookmakers who were terrorised by the Elephant Mob.

The mutual hatred between the Elephant Mob and the Sabini Gang came to a head in 1927 outside the Duke of Wellington pub. Both gangs were armed with pistols and shotguns plus a variety of knives.

After obscenities were exchanged between Sabini and McDonald the fight was on. Thirty minutes eight gang members were dead; bleeding on the street.

THE AFTERMATH

CHAPTER 31

GANGS

Street gangs have been in existence since time immemorial. In ancient Rome gangs of youths caused havoc on the streets. Cicero references armed bands of young men who engaged in fights disrupting the city for years.

UNITED STATES

It is estimated that in 2018 there was 30,000 gangs with 800,000 members across the USA. An additional 150,000 members were residing in U.S. prisons.

Hispanics accounted for 47% of all gang members. The balance was made up of Blacks 31%, Whites 13% and Asians 6%.

LATIN AMERICA

It is estimated there are 50,000 gang members in El Salvador. The Mexican drug cartels boast over 100,000 gang members.

ASIA

The Yakuza in Japan is one of the largest crime gangs in the world. Their membership tops 90,000.

The Triad in Hong Kong has 160,000 active members.

EUROPE

The Mafia have approximately 25,000 gang members with 250,000 affiliates worldwide.

AUSTRALIA

Australia has a history of street gangs going back to the earliest days of European colonisation. The Rocks Push was the most famous.

In modern times prominent gangs are 5T, a Vietnamese gang and other Asian gangs including Four Aces and Madonna's Mob.

The fastest growing gangs are Middle Eastern.

The most organised gangs are outlaw motorcycle gangs such as Hells Angels, Bandidos and the Gypsy Jokers.

GANGSTERS

Gangsters still rule the streets of Australia's cities.

MELBOURNE
CARL WILLIAMS

Carl Williams was born on 19 October 1970 and grew up in Broadmeadows close by to Eddy McGuire. Both men became rich— one legally and the other from a life of crime.

Williams left school after completing Year 11. Broadmeadows was a working-class suburb but working didn't suit young Carl. His first conviction was for handling stolen goods and failing to answer bail. He received a $400 fine.

Carl and his elder brother were very close. Carl was devastated when Shane died from a drug overdose in 1997. He married convicted drug dealer Roberta Mercieca soon after they had a daughter, Dhakota, in March 2001.

Carl tried his hand at various labouring jobs, but hard physical work didn't suit him.

Roberta and Carl opened a children's clothing store but the venture failed.

There had to be a better way: and there was.

Carl and his father were arrested for drug trafficking. They were found with 25,000 amphetamine tablets in their possession. The estimated value was $20 million.

Having lost his brother to an overdose he lost his mother to suicide in 2008.

Jason Moran shot Williams in the abdomen. Why? Because he owed the Moran family $80,000. Let the war begin.

2002 - Williams hired hitman Andrew Veniamin as his wingman.

15 June - 2000 Mark Moran, Jason's brother, was shot and killed outside his home.

Williams was charged with his murder but the charges were dropped when a deal was cut with the police. Carl pleaded guilty of other murders.

21 June 2003 – Jason Moran and his gangster mate, Pasquale Barbaro, were sitting in the front of a people mover. Their children, all five, were sitting in the back. They were to watch the kids train for football which had just finished.

A gunman approached and killed both Moran and Barbaro with a handgun and a shotgun. They both died instantly, leaving the children in shock. They would probably suffer from PSTD for the rest of their lives.

Many other gangland murders occurred over the coming years including Lewis Moran, the patriarch of the family.

28 February 2007 – Carl Lewis pleaded guilty to several murders. He was sentenced to life in prison.

While in prison he turned informant. His reward was that the Victorian Government would pay for his daughter's private school fees.

19 April 2010 - Williams was incarcerated in the high security Barwon Prison when his cell mate Mathew Johnson used the stem of an exercise bike to bash Williams to death. His funeral was held on 30 April at St Therese's Catholic Church in Essendon.

Alphonse Gangito deceased gangland murder
Tony Mokbel serving thirty years in prison
Jason Moran deceased gangland murder
Lewis Moran deceased gangland murder
Crime doesn't pay

SYDNEY

Sydney in the eighties was a cesspit of crime run by gangsters with the help of corrupt police.

NEDDY SMITH

None was more evil than Neddy Smith. Life started for Neddy as an illegitimate baby born to a mother who had four children to four separate men. Neddy's father was an American sailor whom Neddy never got to meet.

Neddy's life in institutions began at an early age he was placed in a boys' home after being caught stealing.

His life of incarceration continued. His first prison sentence began with a three-year stint when he was nineteen. This was followed by a seven-year sentence. His last and final stay began in 1989. He died in prison in 2021.

Neddy was an imposing figure who stood six feet six inches tall and weighed approximately 102 kg. He used his impressive frame to intimidate and bash various opponents.

His criminal career included heroin dealing, armed robbery and murder. Neddy knew how to fight. He was credited with beating a former Commonwealth heavyweight champion.

Neddy had a gang in his corner. It wasn't your normal gang— although he did command a group of thugs— it was the gang of corrupt police.

The cops would not only turn a blind eye to Neddy's indiscretions such as robberies, heroin dealing and murder, but they would set up targets for him.

Smith was credited with nine murders but convicted of only two. He became a whistle-blower at the ICAC hearings (Commission Against Corruption).

He testified that he had committed eight armed robberies and made millions from heroin dealing. He was given immunity on all charges except murder if he testified against corrupt cop Roger Rogerson and the other corrupt police officers that were on his payroll.

Neddy remained at Long Bay until his death. He had suffered from Parkinson's disease for many years.

OTHER SYDNEY GANGSTERS

George Freeman: Died from natural causes
Michael Kanaan: Serving fifty years for multiple murders
Lenny McPherson: Jailed for life for multiple murders. Died from a heart attack in jail.
Abraham Saffron: Died from natural causes.

Most countries have their fair share of gangsters, from Hisayuki in Tokyo to Amado Fuentes in Mexico.

It surely is the oldest profession in the world.

THE END

BIBLIOGRAPHY

Biography – Matilda Mary (Tilly) Devine – ...

w Tilly Devine – Wikipedia

🗋 1st Aust Tunnelling Co |

🗋 History of Camberwell | London Borough ...

👑 History of London – 20th century London

📷 View digital copy

Obituary – James Edward (Jim) Devine – O...

🗋 Matilda Mary "Tilly Devine" Twiss Parsons (...

G Razor (Underbelly) – Larry Writer – Google...

▶ Razor (Underbelly) – Google Play

w Kate Leigh – Wikipedia

🗋 The 1920s: the Razor Wars | Sydney Crim...

🗋 Tilly Devine & the Razor Gang Wars – Stat...

w Razor gang – Wikipedia

🗋 The 1930s: Phil Jeffs – Sydney Crime Muse...

Biography – Phillip (Phil) Jeffs – People Au...

Melbourne gangster Norman Bruhn smell...

Life Summary – Norman Bruhn – Obituari...

Khaki Crims and Desperadoes by Russell ...

Details

6th Australian Infantry Battalion | The Aus...

🗋 veo-download

Obituary – Norman Bruhn – Obituaries Au...

Ellen Catherine "Nellie Cameron" Kelly Bo...

a The Rise and Fall of Squizzy Taylor: A larri...

Kindle Cloud Reader

Cockney Capones who ran London | UK n...

The real Peaky Blinders: Victorian gang w...

w Charles Sabini – Wikipedia

w Peaky Blinders – Wikipedia

w Elephant and Castle Mob – Wikipedia

B CaseBook: Birmingham gang leader at cen...

w List of mobsters by city – Wikipedia

w Gang – Wikipedia

w Gangs in Australia – Wikipedia

Gang | crime | Britannica.com

w Mohocks – Wikipedia

Top 15 Crime Bosses and Drug Lords in 2...

"normal" or socially acceptable behaviou

Acknowledgements

Preview Readers

Ian Jones
Martin Humphreys
Jan Blakeborough

Edit Sally Odgers

First published 2022 by Crabtree Pty Ltd

Gangsters & Whores is a work of fiction. Any resemblance to real persons, living or dead, is purely coincidental.

ISBN: 978-0-6451166-6-3 (p/b)
ISBN: 978-0-6451166-7-0 (ebook)